"I was trying to make you mad."

Leah jerked. *"What?"*

Henry's lips shifted into a gentle smile. "While you were angry, you forgot about the storm."

Her anger left as quickly as it had come. "You knew I was terrified."

"Ja."

She blushed. "I didn't want you to see."

The good humor left his expression. "I understand."

Leah stared at him and wondered if he *did* understand, but she didn't want to discuss her fear anymore, and she prayed and hoped that he would keep her weakness to himself. "You won't tell anyone?"

He appeared confused. "About—"

"That I'm a coward and deathly afraid of thunderstorms."

His eyes widened. "You're no coward, Leah. A coward wouldn't have run out into the storm to see her horse to safety."

Leah blinked, pleased by his words.

"I'll not say a word about today, Leah." Henry looked sad, and Leah struggled with the urge to do something to make his sadness go away. "No one will know that you spend any time here with me in the store. Your secret is safe."

Rebecca Kertz was first introduced to the Amish when her husband took a job with an Amish construction crew. She enjoyed watching the Amish foreman's children at play and swapping recipes with his wife. Rebecca resides in Delaware with her husband and dog. She has a strong faith in God and feels blessed to have family nearby. Besides writing, she enjoys reading, doing crafts and visiting Lancaster County.

Books by Rebecca Kertz

Love Inspired

Women of Lancaster County

A Secret Amish Love
Her Amish Christmas Sweetheart
Her Forgiving Amish Heart

Lancaster County Weddings

Noah's Sweetheart
Jedidiah's Bride
A Wife for Jacob
Elijah and the Widow
Loving Isaac

Lancaster Courtships

The Amish Mother

Her Forgiving Amish Heart

Rebecca Kertz

LOVE INSPIRED BOOKS

ISBN-13: 978-1-335-50959-8

Her Forgiving Amish Heart

This edition published by arrangement with Love Inspired Books.

www.Harlequin.com

Printed in U.S.A.

Chapter One

Late spring, Lancaster County, Pennsylvania

She felt the first drops of rain as she steered her horse-drawn open wagon home after a visit to her friend Mary. Leah Stoltzfus sighed as she reached under the carriage seat for her umbrella. She probably should have headed home hours ago, but it had been so nice to spend time with Mary, who'd fallen in love and married Ethan Bontrager before moving into the house her husband owned in New Holland two years ago.

The light drizzle turned into a shower as Leah pushed open the umbrella while she continued to steer her horse. The patter of rain on fabric was soothing, and she smiled as she made a left turn. She was still miles away from home, but the downpour didn't bother her. Until suddenly the wind picked up, so strong that it turned the umbrella inside out, ruining her rain covering beyond hope. She cried out when a gust tore off her prayer *kapp*. She tried to catch it, but it was a lost cause. When a sharp clap of thunder followed a bright flash of lightning, she knew she was in trouble. She needed to find a safe place to wait out the storm. She sent up a silent prayer that the Lord help her to find shelter soon. She had been terrified of thunderstorms since being caught in a severe one as a young child.

Yoder's General Store loomed ahead as if the Lord had provided in Leah's time of need. Relieved, she pulled into the parking lot and tied up her horse before she ran to the front entrance. Thunder rattled the building's windows as she tugged to open the door, but it wouldn't budge.

Locked! A flash of lightning made her flinch. The rain spilled down in buckets now, and the air temperature dropped quickly. Soaked, she hugged herself with her arms as she tried to keep calm. The wind gusted and blew the rain sideways while lightning continued to flash and was followed by horrific crashes of thunder.

Feeling desperate, Leah leaned her face against the window to peer inside and caught a tiny flicker of light from the back room. *Thanks be to God!* She hurried around to the rear entrance and hammered on the door with her fist. She waited for someone to come, her heart racing wildly as she tried not to shrink with fear every time there was lightning and thunder. She pounded again. *Please, Lord. Please, Lord.*

What was she going to do? Worried about her horse, she turned to leave.

The door flew open behind her. "Leah?" a male voice roared above the wind. "Is that you?"

She spun, then stared at the man who gazed at her from the open doorway. Henry Yoder. The last person she'd expected to see—and the last man she wanted anything to do with. He unsettled her. He'd once been her cousin Isaac's best friend, until he'd betrayed him.

"I have to go." She gasped. A boom of thunder made her duck for cover, her arms shielding her head.

"Leah." His voice was soft and near. "Come in from the rain." He captured her arm gently and pulled her into the store.

Leah was tempted to stay, her fear momentarily getting the better of her. Then she met Henry's gaze and closed her eyes, debating. Storm versus Henry Yoder. She bucked up as she made the choice to rein in her fear. She sprang out the door.

"Leah!" he shouted as he came out after her.

She halted and met his concerned gaze. "My mare."

Understanding brightened his blue eyes. He nodded. "We'll put her in the storage barn. I'll get your buggy."

She shook her head, refusing to allow him to see how frightened she was. "I'll get it."

Their gazes locked. Henry stared at her, then inclined his head. "I'll meet you over there." He gestured toward the large pole-barn structure behind the store, then rushed out into the blinding rain after shutting the door behind him.

Water streamed in her eyes as she ran to her buggy. Her horse was antsy, shifting nervously as she whinnied. Concerned for the animal despite her fear, she took the time to stroke the animal's neck. "I'm going to get you inside where it's safe, girl."

After one last pat, she lifted a leg to climb into the vehicle, slipping on the wet wood before she managed to get seated. Leah grabbed the leathers and steered the horse toward the Yoders' outbuilding. Her heart gave a lurch when she saw that Henry had dragged open the two huge doors for her. He stood back and waved her into the building, but as she urged the mare closer, he grabbed hold of its halter and led her horse inside. The interior of the structure was dark except for the brief flashes of lightning that lit it up. Leah waited until he maneuvered her vehicle in as far as it could go before she let go of her tight hold on the reins and climbed down. Henry waited for her at the rear of the buggy.

"'Tis a little noisy, but she will be safe here," he said. Rain plastered his dark hair to his head. Rivulets of water ran down his handsome face and his clothes were soaked, but he didn't seem to mind. "Come on. Let's get back to the store."

Leah opened her mouth to refuse, to tell him that she would wait with her wagon inside the building, but then she closed it and nodded. She couldn't be rude to Henry after he'd come to her aid. Besides, she wasn't going to let the man see her as anyone other than a strong-minded individual who wasn't fazed by anything. *Especially by him.* Bright lightning flashed, followed by a thunderous boom. She gasped. *Except by thunderstorms.*

A bright white bolt shot from the sky, and there was an explosion as it hit something in the distance. "Come on!" Henry urged. "Let's go now before things get worse." She was shocked, conscious of the warmth of his fingers when he caught her hand and tugged her with him as he ran.

Aware of Leah's hand in his, Henry hurried to safety. The storm was a doozy. It had been a long time since he'd seen one this bad. He pulled open the door, tugged her inside, then shoved the door shut against a gust of wind.

"Are you *oll recht*?" he asked when he saw how hard

Whoso findeth a wife findeth a good thing,
and obtaineth favour of the Lord.
—*Proverbs* 18:22

For Judith E. French, my dearest friend
and the sister of my heart. You touched
my life in ways you'll never know. Thank you
for everything. Our friendship of nearly
thirty-six years has meant a lot to me.
May you rest in peace, dear Judy. I love you.

she was breathing. Her eyes refused to meet his as she inclined her head. A crack of thunder made her flinch, and he reached for her and eased her away from the door. He flipped on the light in the storage room and urged her inside.

She glanced at him with alarm that told him she was as afraid of him as she was the storm. Hurt, he hid his reaction and softened his expression. "'Tis safer here," he explained. He gave her a crooked smile. "No windows."

Understanding flickered in her eyes and he was glad to see her relax.

She shivered. He realized that she was cold, soaked through like he was. "I'll be right back," he said. He hurried to the front of the store. Behind the counter hung a quilt made by his mother. His *mam* had hoped to sell it, but with the Amish as their main customers there was little opportunity for a sale, so it hung high on the wall simply as a decoration. Henry reached up, slipped it from the wall rack and returned to the storage room. He caught sight of Leah, off guard, hugging herself with her arms. She was bent forward as if she could shield herself from the raging storm outside.

He felt a painful lurch in his chest as he studied her without her knowledge. Wet blond hair, the bluest eyes and prettiest face he'd ever seen, Leah Stoltzfus was something to behold even as clearly upset as she was. He longed to pull her into his arms to comfort her, but from the look on her face when he'd answered the door, he knew she wouldn't welcome his hug. She'd wanted to flee when she saw him and he understood why. Years ago Leah's cousin Isaac and he had befriended some young *Englishers* during their time of *rumspringa*. Late one night, while Henry waited for Isaac to join them, Brad Smith and his English friends had spray-painted graffiti over the exterior of Whittier's Store. When Isaac had arrived on the scene, Brad had shoved a can of spray paint into Isaac's hands, then dragged Henry with him as he fled while the sound of police sirens echoed in the distance. Brad had warned Henry against telling the authorities who was responsible and promised retribution against him, his family and Isaac if Henry did. This new side of Brad had terrified him, and so Henry had kept his mouth shut and allowed his best friend to take the blame. Isaac had stayed silent and suffered because of it. Henry had waited too long before he'd finally come forward, confessed before the church congregation and asked for forgiveness. The community had forgiven him and so had Isaac. But given her cousin's suffering because of Henry, and the fact that Leah had avoided him ever since, he didn't think she had forgiven him.

Henry sighed with disappointment before he eased back to where she couldn't see him. He made a loud sound to give her warning of his return. With the quilt draped over his arm, he entered.

"Here," he said as he approached. He tried unsuccessfully not to be offended when she instinctively backed away. He exhaled loudly. "Leah, 'tis just something to warm you."

Her eyes flickered as she saw what he held. "I'm sorry." He saw her swallow hard. "I…I'm not exactly fond of thunderstorms." She seemed surprised by her admission.

He smiled as he moved closer, relieved that she didn't withdraw as he draped the quilt gently around her shoulders. He gazed at her and she stared back. The room was small, and he could see her fear of the storm in her pretty blue eyes, hear it in her heightened breathing, although he could tell she was struggling to fight it. "Are you warmer now?"

"Ja, danki." She glanced away.

"I don't bite, Leah."

Her head came up and anger lit her expression. "You think that's funny?"

Holding her gaze, he shook his head. *"Nay."* He was glad to see her angry and less afraid.

"How long will this storm go on?" she complained after another clap of thunder reverberated throughout the store.

"Are you asking me for an answer?" he quipped with amusement.

He felt happy when Leah narrowed her gaze at him. Anger was so much better than fear. She'd endure the storm better if he continued to taunt and tease, keeping her fury alive.

"What are you doing out in the storm anyway, Leah?" he asked.

"I was—" She stopped. "What business of it is yours?" she snapped.

Henry shrugged. "None, I guess. I'm just curious." He leaned casually back against a stack of cardboard boxes filled with merchandise. "Doesn't seem smart to venture out in a storm so far from home."

She opened and closed her mouth several times, clearly trying to come up with a retort. Her lips firmed. He hid his pleasure when her eyes shot daggers at him. "It wasn't storming when I left this morning for New Holland," she replied through tight lips.

"You went to see Mary and Ethan Bontrager."

She looked shocked. "How did you know?"

He was starting to feel uncomfortable with his wet hair and soaked clothes. "I know that you and Mary are friends and Mary married Ethan, then moved to New Holland."

She looked horrified. "How do you know who my friends are? You've not been coming to church services or any Visiting Sundays!"

"*Ja*, but I'm friends with Isaac."

"Isaac and you are spending time together?" She gasped.

He had to stifle his own spark of anger. "*Ja*, your cousin has forgiven me as the other members of the community have." He paused. "Except for you."

Her eyes widened as she gazed up at him. She was obviously at a loss on how to respond. He detected a flash of remorse in her eyes before she looked away. The fact that she didn't deny it hurt. "I forgave you," she mumbled, looking away.

Skeptical, he pushed away from the boxes. "I'm going to check outside. See how the storm is doing." He hoped it would be on its way out, for it hurt to endure Leah's judgment of him. He strode out of the storage room toward the back entrance. He opened the door and released a sharp breath when he saw the pouring rain. He detected a brightening in the sky that told him the worst of the storm has passed. The distant rumble of thunder confirmed it. The thunderstorm had moved on, leaving only rain. The wind had left as quickly as it'd blown in.

Henry shut the door. He wasn't eager to return to the storage room. He'd lived with the guilt of what he'd done long enough. He didn't need Leah Stoltzfus reminding him of his past mistakes. He still felt bad enough as it was. He moved to the window to stare at the rain until it slowed, then finally stopped.

Henry was gone a long time. It shouldn't bother her but it did. Leah listened and realized that she could no longer hear thunder. The small room where she stood had muffled the storm and she felt less frightened. Or was it her fury at Henry that had caused her to forget the storm?

Should she wait for his return? She closed her eyes. She wouldn't blame him if he didn't come back. She'd been awful to him, and she felt bad about it.

He and Isaac talked about me? And just like that her anger returned. She closed her eyes and prayed. Anger was a sin. She needed to fight it.

'Tis not right to be angry or deliberately cruel to a man who helped me when I needed aid most.

She didn't know how to deal with Henry Yoder—or any man for that matter. She'd never had a sweetheart, never had any man's attention and her at nearly twenty-four years of age.

Leah closed her eyes. Resigned to being an old maid, she would choose her own future. She ran her fingers across the multicolored quilt that Henry had given her. The pattern was lovely, the stitches neat and even. She always appreciated good craftsmanship. One day, she'd open a craft store where she'd stock quilts just like this one. She'd use the money she'd earned and saved for years, sewing prayer *kapps* and clothes for other church community members, and making craft items and selling them wherever she could. She also did mending for a few of the women who said they were too busy. It wouldn't matter if she didn't have a husband and children. She would focus on her dream and she would be happy. With the Lord's help, she'd find the peace and enjoyment in being a store owner—and she wouldn't let it upset her that her father never urged her to find a husband like he did with her sisters. He'd pushed her older sister, Nell, to find a husband first—which she did, although the fact that he was an *Englisher* had been a problem at first. Then, there was Meg. Three years younger than her, Meg was happily married to Peter Zook, a nice young man and member of their church community. As for her other younger sisters Ellie and Charlie, there was plenty of time for them to find sweethearts, although she'd witnessed firsthand the attention that the community boys gave them. She knew they would marry and have families of their own, even if she never did.

Which bought her thoughts back to Henry Yoder. The only man who had shown her kindness—for a little while anyway. His snarky attitude afterward just confirmed that she wasn't worth any man's attention.

She scowled. Not that she would ever like Henry Yoder. The man couldn't be trusted. She had forgiven him for what he'd done to Isaac. But forget? *Never.*

Leah wondered how long she should stay in the room. Was Henry upset enough to leave her there? To lock up the store and go home? And what would she do if he did? How would she get her horse and wagon? Were the pole-barn doors locked? Would she be able to slide them open if they weren't? Panic set in and she had trouble catching her breath. She recognized her symptoms as hyperventilation, having suffered from it once before. Yet, she was powerless to help herself.

"Leah, the rain's stopped." Henry entered as she struggled to slow her breathing. She heard him utter an exclamation and saw him rush out of the room. He returned within minutes with a paper bag. "Leah," he coaxed softly, "breathe into this."

She looked up with relief as she took it and held it over her nose and mouth. She closed her eyes and breathed deeply into the bag until she was able to draw a normal breath. She could sense Henry's presence, feel his concern. She was a terrible person. The man had been there for her twice, and she'd snapped at him like a shrew.

Slowly she opened her eyes and faced him. Henry studied her with concern, which eased when she pulled the bag from her mouth. He was taller than her by several inches. She looked up at him with remorse. "I'm sorry."

He frowned. "What for?"

"My behavior." For some reason, her voice was hoarse and she didn't know why.

The grin that curved up his mouth lit up his face and sky blue eyes. "Leah," he said, "I was trying to make you mad."

She jerked. *"What?"*

His lips shifted into a gentle smile. "While you were livid, you forgot about the storm."

Her anger left as quickly as it had come. "You knew I was terrified," she said softly.

"Ja."

She blushed. "I didn't want you to see."

The good humor left his expression. "I understand."

Leah stared at him and wondered if he *did* understand, but she didn't want to discuss her fear anymore, and she prayed and hoped that he would keep her weakness to himself. "You won't tell anyone?"

He appeared confused. "About—"

"That I'm a coward and deathly afraid of thunderstorms."

His eyes widened. "You're no coward, Leah. A coward wouldn't have run out into the storm to see her horse to safety."

Leah blinked, pleased by his words.

"I'll not say a word about today, Leah." Henry looked sad, and Leah struggled with the urge to do something to make his sadness go away. "No one will know that you spent any time here with me in the store. Your secret is safe."

And for some odd reason, Leah felt dejected as he preceded her out of the room, then out of the store… and as she watched him open the barn doors for her and waited for her to get into her wagon. As she steered her buggy home, the feeling intensified and tears stung her eyes. She had no idea why she was so emotional about taking shelter during a thunderstorm.

Henry stood near the barn and watched Leah leave. His thoughts were in turmoil. Everyone in the community had forgiven him for keeping silent except Leah Stoltzfus—and himself. Despite his hurt feelings, he liked being in Leah's company. She was a mystery that he wanted to unravel. It was true that he hadn't been back to her church community. His family had left after learning about Isaac's involvement in the vandalism to Whittier's Store. His father didn't want Isaac to be a bad influence, which made him feel worse. After he'd come forward and confessed and told the truth about

Isaac's innocence before Leah's church community, his parents had been so horrified by Henry's involvement that they'd felt compelled to stay with their new church district. Despite the new people he'd met, he missed his friends. Isaac had been more than generous in his forgiveness of him. They were close friends again, and Henry could never repay Isaac enough for thinking to protect him by accepting blame.

He'd wanted for a long time to return to the church community he'd been a part of for most of his life. He wanted to see the Lapps every Sunday, to spend more time with Isaac and his siblings, and the Zooks and all of the other families he'd known and cared about. After this afternoon he wanted to see and spend time with Leah again. One way or another he'd find a way to make her forgive him—and like him. There was something about the woman that made his heart race. She made him feel alive. From the moment he'd seen her outside the door, he'd known who she was. He was glad that he'd been there to make sure she was all right. He'd liked helping her, wished he could have done more.

Henry went back inside. He peeked into the storage room, saw the damp quilt that he'd placed around her shoulders and felt the kick to his belly caused by her absence. He'd caught her stroking the stitches along the pattern as if she appreciated the quilt and all the work that had gone into it. There was something about her expression that got to him. He wanted to learn all of her secrets. "I'm going to make you like me, Leah Stoltzfus, if it's the last thing I do."

He draped the damp quilt over the counter to dry, then flipped off the light and went back into the rear room to finish the store's bookkeeping. This building was the only one on the property with electricity. The church elders allowed it in certain businesses, although not in their homes and outbuildings. Cell phones were allowed for business use, but his parents were opposed to them so Yoder's General Store didn't have one. Henry knew that would have to change if they were ever to increase their business to include more of the English. Until then he'd keep his mouth shut and work in the store. He had a dream of his own and it wasn't to take over the family business. But he stifled that dream because he owed it to his parents for all the trouble he'd caused them. Now, with his father suddenly in the hospital and his mother spending her days at his bedside, it was up to him to make sure Yoder's General Store ran smoothly as usual.

Someday, if the Lord deemed it, he would have his choice of making a living—as a cabinetmaker. Not in competition with Noah Lapp, who had a good business crafting quality furniture. But similar to what Ethan Bontrager did for a living in New Holland, making kitchen cabinets, vanities and bookcases. He and Isaac had spent some time in Noah's furniture shop. He'd loved feeling the texture of the wood, instinctively knowing that he'd be good at cabinetry.

Henry grinned as he recalled Leah's reaction to his comment about her and Mary Bontrager. Isaac and he had never discussed Leah's friendship with Mary. He knew because he'd seen them together often enough when he'd attended church service or Visiting Sunday gatherings. Isaac and he had talked about Henry's secret desire for his future, and Isaac had mentioned that Mary Hershberger Bontrager's husband, Ethan, made cabinets for a living. His friend had suggested that Henry talk with Ethan about the business. Henry had planned to visit Ethan the next day, but then his father's recent heart attack had changed everything. He'd visited *Dat* in the hospital, where his parents had made him promise to run the store. Henry had agreed. Being a dutiful son was the least he could do for the parents who'd raised and loved him.

Unable to be or do what he wanted didn't mean he couldn't make the best out of a difficult situation. He'd keep the store open. *And I'll convince Leah to forgive me.* He smiled as he looked forward to the challenge.

Chapter Two

Her family was relieved to see Leah as she steered the wagon into the yard and parked it near the barn. They were all outside, as if hoping that the buggy sound they'd heard was her. She climbed down from the vehicle and faced them.

"Leah!" *Mam* said as she hurried forward, quickly followed by Ellie and Charlie. "I was worried that you'd been caught in the storm." Her eyes widened as she took in Leah's appearance—the damp state of her clothes, her missing prayer *kapp* and wet hair.

"*Ja*, I was caught at first but managed to find shelter." Leah smiled to reassure her and her sisters as she watched her father descend the front porch and approach more slowly. He looked more concerned than her mother. "As you can see, I'm fine." She met her father's gaze as he drew close. *"Dat."*

"Leah." He studied her as if gauging whether or not she was all right, then he seemed to let go of his worry. "I'm glad you're home."

"I am, too, *Dat*." She moved toward the house and

everyone fell into step with her. "I'm hungry, though. 'Tis been a long time since lunch."

"Supper is nearly ready," her mother said, moving ahead, apparently eager to get the meal on the table.

"We're having fried chicken," Charlie added with delight. She hurried to help her mother.

Leah turned to Ellie. "Were you caught in it?" she asked her sister.

"*Nay.* Got home just in the nick of time." Ellie eyed her carefully. "'Twas a bad one."

"Ja," she agreed.

"Ellie, you should help your *mudder*."

"Ja, Dat." Leah watched her sister run into the house. She turned toward her father.

"Dochter," he said.

"Ja?"

"Was it awful?"

She knew what he meant. He was asking how well she'd coped with her fear. He was the only one who knew of her phobia. He was the one who'd found her during a raging storm curled up in a ball in an open field, sobbing with terror as thunder crashed overhead and lightning flashed while it threatened to strike her. He'd picked her up and carried her to safety. Despite the fact they were walking through the storm to the nearest shelter in their barn, she'd felt safe and secure within his arms. She was three years old at the time. Her mother hadn't been home. *Mam* and her older sister, Nell, were at her grandparents' house. As young as she'd been, Leah had begged her father that no one learn of what happened. Her father had agreed readily. Her mother was with Meg, and he hadn't wanted to upset her. And so they'd both kept the knowledge—

and Leah's subsequent fear of thunderstorms—to themselves. As far as she knew, she hid her fear well and her family still didn't know.

"Nay," she said and realized that she spoke the truth. "I did *gut*." Despite her initial terror, she'd weathered the storm better than usual—because of Henry Yoder. She felt worse than ever before for treating him badly.

Her father's expression cleared. "That's wonderful, Leah." His smile reached his eyes. "Let's go eat supper."

Surrounded by her parents and sisters at the dinner table, Leah felt the stress of being caught in the storm and her time spent with Henry dissipate. She smiled as she listened idly to her youngest sister Charlotte's conversation with Ellie.

"Visiting Day is at Aunt Katie and Uncle Samuel's," Charlie said. "Can we bring chowchow and apple pie?"

Ellie arched her eyebrows. "Why chowchow? I'm sure Aunt Katie has plenty."

Charlie frowned. "Who says she'll serve hers?" Then softly, as if voicing her thoughts, she murmured too quietly for the others to hear, except for Leah who sat next to her, "I want to bring something I made by myself."

Leah shot her a look and noted the wistfulness in Charlie's expression. She smiled in Ellie's direction. "I think it's a great idea for us to bring chowchow. The last batch was the best I've ever tasted." She could feel Charlie's gratitude in the release of tension in her sister's shoulders. "I'm sure Aunt Katie only brings hers out if no one else thinks to bring some."

"That's true," her mother said with a smile. "So, we'll bring chowchow, and I'll make the apple pie and some sweet-and-vinegar green beans. Any other ideas?"

"I'll make potato salad," Leah offered.

Ellie grinned. “I’ll make a cake.”

“I’ll help you with the cake,” Charlie offered, clearly happy that everyone had agreed that they should bring a bowl of her sweet-and-sour chowchow, a pickled mixture of the remainder of last summer’s garden vegetables, a favorite among the members of their Amish community.

The next morning Leah worked to make German potato salad while Ellie and Charlie gathered the ingredients to make a cake and her mother rolled dough for an apple pie. She loved these times when the women in her family were all together in the kitchen, but she missed having her married sisters, Nell and Meg, with them.

As she carefully drained the hot water off the potatoes, Leah found her thoughts drifting to Henry and his kindness to her during yesterday’s thunderstorm. The last thing she’d wanted to do was spend time with him, but he’d made it bearable. She’d found herself softening when he’d wrapped a quilt around her shoulders. Leah frowned. She didn’t want to think of Henry. It bothered her that she’d been unable to get him out of her thoughts since she’d left the store.

Forcing Henry from her mind, she concentrated on enjoying the time with her mother and sisters while she made her potato salad and found happiness in the company of her family.

Sunday morning Leah got ready to spend Visiting Day at her Lapp relatives. Once she’d put aside thoughts of the storm—and Henry—the day spent with her mother and sisters baking and cooking was wonderful. Amish women weren’t allowed to cook or do any work on Sundays, so it was important to make sure everything was done by Saturday afternoon. Leah had made two large bowls of German potato salad, a family favorite. Ellie and Charlie had baked two cakes, one chocolate and one carrot. *Mam* had baked the apple pie and made traditional sweet-and-sour green beans with sugar, vinegar and chopped pieces of cooked bacon. The green beans fixed this way were delicious cold as well as hot, so it was the perfect side dish to any Sunday meal.

Since Friday's thunderstorm, she'd been unable to keep Henry Yoder out of her mind. Would he be visiting with Isaac today? Her heart thumped hard at the thought. She wished she'd taken the extra time to thank him, as well as apologize for the way she'd been eager to get away from him. Thinking on it a lot since then, Leah realized that Henry made her nervous. No man ever affected her that way. She shouldn't continue to fret about it but found it difficult to stop.

It was a perfect spring day, with temperatures well into the upper seventies. As her father steered their family buggy close to the Samuel Lapp house, Leah noticed that everyone was outside enjoying the weather. Tables were set up on the back lawn and her male cousins were already playing baseball in the side yard. She felt a burst of excitement as she climbed out of the parked buggy and reached in to grab the two bowls of potato salad. It looked to be a good time spent with good people. Charlie and Ellie joined her as she watched the activity about the house.

"Do you think *Endie* Katie wants us to bring the food inside?" Charlie asked.

"Ja," Leah said. "'Tis too early for lunch and we didn't bring any breakfast foods."

"There's she is now!" Ellie exclaimed. "Let's ask her."

Mam and *Dat* appeared beside them as they headed to greet Leah's aunt. Her uncle Samuel came out of the house behind his wife, and Leah watched as they talked a moment. The affection between the two wasn't overt, but she could see the love they shared in the way they regarded each other—and the way her uncle placed a hand gently for a moment on her aunt's shoulder. Leah felt a little twinge of pain as she realized she wanted a relationship like they had. She wanted a husband and a family. She straightened her spine. If the Lord wanted her to marry, then she would. If not, then she must be content with only a craft business in her future. She'd find joy in her shop and be grateful for her loving family and her friends. She had no right to feel anything else.

"*Endie* Katie!" Charlie exclaimed with a grin as her aunt and uncle approached. "We've got apple pie, cake, chowchow, green beans, and Leah made her German potato salad!"

"So much food," Katie said, beaming. "Are you hoping to feed our entire community?"

When her aunt looked in her direction, Leah smiled. "Better too much than not enough."

"Do you want everything in the kitchen?" *Mam* asked.

"*Ja*, that would be *gut*." Katie turned to her brother. "*Hallo*, Arlin. I'm glad you're here."

Her *dat* eyed his sister with affection. "I wouldn't miss this." His voice softened. "I still thank the Lord that we moved home."

"*Ja*. Happiness is a fine place to live," Missy agreed. "I'm more than content to live here."

Her father shot his wife a grateful look. Leah loved watching her parents together. There was so much love between her mother and father and her relatives with their spouses that she was pleased to be a part of the family. Not for the first time, she silently thanked the Lord for the blessings He'd given her throughout her life.

"Charlie!" a male voice called. "Want to play baseball?" It was their cousin Joseph Lapp. He tossed the ball back and forth between his hands. "I need someone *gut* on my team."

Charlie laughed. "Aren't you afraid I'll show you up?"

Joseph shot her a grin. "Not if you're on my team."

"Let me put these cakes inside the house and then I'll play."

Leah laughed when she heard Joseph's older brothers groan. "Not fair, Joseph. She's younger than us," Daniel complained.

On her way to the house, her youngest sister halted. "Already making excuses, cousin?"

The other members of Joseph's team chuckled. "Sounds about right, Daniel," Joseph said.

"Our teams will be even. You'll be able to play now." Joseph looked toward a spot out of Leah's sight.

She froze when she recognized the dark-haired man as he stepped into her view. *Henry Yoder.* She stared at him, and he locked gazes with her. She noted the upward quirk of his lips. Her face heated as she felt a sudden spirt of irritation. He hadn't come because he wanted to see her, had he? He arched an eyebrow as if reading her thoughts and she looked away. When she glanced back, she saw Isaac join him. The two men talked, and Isaac laughed at something Henry said.

He'd better not be talking about me!

Flushed with outrage, Leah continued to the house. Henry's presence made her feel unsettled. All thoughts of apologizing to him vanished. She scowled. She could hide in the house, but she was no fool. He'd know immediately why she was avoiding him, and as he'd told her she was no coward.

He knew when he heard Joseph call her sister Charlie's name that Leah would be close by. But seeing her again, despite the unhappiness in her expression as she glared at him, buoyed his spirits. He'd hoped she'd be here today, figured she would be since the Lapps were her family, but he couldn't be sure. He hid a grin. She was upset to see him. He must have affected her more than he'd realized.

"I don't think your cousin likes me," he said to Isaac.

Isaac frowned. "Which one?"

"Leah."

"*Nay*, not possible. Leah likes everyone. What makes you think she doesn't?"

Henry's gaze followed Leah as she headed toward the house. "She glares at me."

His friend laughed. "You're imagining things."

"*Nay.* She hasn't forgiven me for what I did to you."

Isaac frowned. "That doesn't sound like her."

"Look at her. See for yourself."

Leah had paused to glance back.

"She does look unhappy with you." Isaac grew thoughtful. "Interesting." He met Henry's gaze. "Ellie told me that Leah wants to open a craft shop. Maybe you could offer to help her. You know about running a store and keeping books. She might soften toward you while you teach her all you know."

Henry brightened and felt a sudden shifting inside of him. "That might work."

"But be careful how you ask her," Isaac warned. "Find time alone with her. Don't let anyone hear about your offer or she's liable to get mad and feel as if you're forcing her hand. Besides, not many people know about her store plans."

"I'll be careful."

"I know." Isaac grinned. "You want Leah to like you? This might just be the way to do it."

"What if she refuses my offer?"

"Then you try again later."

"I don't want to force her," Henry said.

"You won't force her. You'll make the offer, then step back. From what Ellie says, Leah wants to own a craft shop badly." Isaac glanced toward the gathering on the lawn. "The others are waiting. Ready to play ball?"

He nodded. As he joined the Lapp brothers and their friends for a baseball game, Henry wondered if Isaac was right. Would teaching Leah about running a store be the key to winning her friendship?

"Henry, you take left field," Joseph shouted from first base. "Charlie, you play short stop."

He nodded and hurried to take his position. There was nothing else to do right now but focus on the game. He'd figure out later what to do with Leah.

The baseball game was fun, with a lot of whooping and hollering as teammates ran around the bases. When he got up to bat, Henry hit a grand slam and sprinted around the bases, sending everyone before him home. As he slid onto home plate, Joseph was there to high-five him. Everyone on his team grinned while taunting those on the opposite side.

"I told you we needed him on our team," Joseph said to two of his brothers and Charlie.

Isaac grinned at him. "'Tis great to play ball together again."

"Are you up for another game?" Noah asked as he and Daniel joined them. Both brothers were on the other team along with the Peachy brothers and Peter Zook.

Joseph laughed. "'Tis lunchtime."

Henry glanced toward the tables that were set up in the yard. "*Ja*, the women are bringing out the food." He felt a rush of pleasure when he spied Leah among them. "Sorry, Noah," he said, unapologetic, as he watched her return to the house. "Food first. Whether or not we have another game will depend on how we feel afterward. Right, team?" He paused. "After all, we've already won. We've nothing to prove."

His teammates laughingly agreed. Henry grinned as they all headed toward the food table. Leah came out of the house with a bowl in each arm. She started forward when she must have heard their laughter. She glanced at him and froze. He slowed his steps. His grin stayed in place as he studied her. She seemed to tense up before she averted her gaze and continued toward the table. She set down the bowls and, without looking back, hurried inside.

The grin faded from Henry's lips. Getting Leah to forgive him wasn't going to be easy. He'd have to find a way to earn her trust first. Friends first, then forgiveness, he thought. Then maybe something more. He froze with shock. *Something more?*

"Hey, you coming?" Isaac asked. "I thought you were hungry."

He smiled at his friend. "I am."

"Let's go then."

The table was overflowing with food. Henry saw cold meats—roast beef, fried chicken and ham. There were a lot of dishes, including a large bowl of macaroni salad, two huge bowls of potato salad, vinegar green beans, dried-corn casserole and many other inviting sides. On a separate table were the desserts. He studied the pies, cakes and other mouthwatering sweets and was glad that Isaac had invited him. His family wasn't here. His mother and father had been invited, too, but even if they were ready to return to their former church district, his *dat's* hospital stay had made it impossible for them to attend. The fact that they probably wouldn't have come if his father had been well made him feel sad and guilty. He had done this to them. Because of what he'd done on *rumspringa*, he'd made it difficult for his parents to face all of these wonderful people.

He was glad that Isaac had invited him. Not only did he get to spend time with everyone, he was able to see Leah Stoltzfus again. Henry sighed as he followed the others to the food table. He could see her, but Leah avoided him like he suffered from the plague. He'd have to be patient. Leah would come out of the house eventually.

Ellen Lapp was among those serving the men and children. Isaac beamed at his wife and Henry gave her a tentative smile. "Henry!" she greeted. "I'm so glad you came."

He relaxed. "I'm happy that Isaac asked me."

"You don't need an invitation—ever," she assured him.

He felt warmth and a fluttering inside his chest. It had been Ellen who'd brought him to his senses and given him the courage to confess what he'd done first to Deacon Abram Peachy, then the rest of the church congregation. *"Danki,"* he whispered.

"Henry, you've got to try my wife's vanilla cream pie." Isaac gestured toward the dessert.

"After you both eat a *gut* meal first," Ellen said with a narrowed but teasing gaze at her husband. She held up a bowl. "German potato salad?" she offered them. "'Tis a favorite. Leah Stoltzfus made it."

Leah made it? He immediately held out his plate. "I don't know that I've ever tasted her potato salad before." As Ellen placed a large scoop on his plate, he discovered that Leah had come out of the house. She was staring at him, and he stared back unflinchingly and arched an eyebrow. She quickly looked away and strode over to where her mother and sisters were talking with Katie Lapp. He hid his amusement. Apparently, he continued to disturb her.

With loaded plate in hand, Henry moseyed on over to where the Stoltzfus women sat. He was eager to test his theory about Leah. "*Hallo.* The food looks *wunderbor*," he said.

Missy, the girls' mother, smiled. "I'm happy you think so."

"I'm particularly eager to try the German potato salad," he commented with a glance in Leah's direction.

"*Ja*, 'tis one of our favorites," Ellie said. "I think you'll enjoy it." She flashed her sister a look. "Leah made it."

"*Hmm.* Can't wait to try it."

Leah eyed him politely. "I suppose you'll let me know whether or not you like it?"

"Absolutely." He smiled. "If you'll excuse me, Isaac is waiting for me." He gestured toward the table filled with married Lapp brothers and their wives. He could sense Leah's gaze on him as he left.

"'Tis *gut* to see him back with us," he heard Missy say.

"Why?" Leah asked stiffly. "Did you miss him?"

"Leah!" her mother scolded.

As he continued toward Isaac's table, Henry couldn't hear Leah's response. But he was secretly pleased. Perhaps her mother could convince Leah that her reaction to him was unreasonable. He hoped so. He'd need her to unbend a little before he approached her with what he hoped was an offer she couldn't refuse. And he'd have to figure out a way to secure a few moments alone with her. He suffered a painful lurch in his belly. He had to do this right or he'd ruin all of his chances of winning the woman's friendship.

"Why would you say such a thing?" Ellie asked, curious.

Leah shrugged, unwilling to admit that she was attracted to Henry Yoder but was afraid to trust him. "Everyone has welcomed him with open arms. It bothers me after the way he hurt Isaac."

"That was a long time ago, Leah." *Mam* made a *tsk* sound with her tongue. "Henry Yoder is a *gut* man. It took a lot of courage to stand before our church congregation and confess. Isaac has forgiven him. Why shouldn't Henry be here? I'm just sorry that Margaret and Harry couldn't come, too."

Blushing, she agreed. "*Ja.* I'm sorry. I'm just feeling out of sorts."

"I'm not the one who deserves an apology." Her mother eyed her with concern. "Are you ill, Leah? 'Tis not like you to be unkind."

"Ja," her sister Meg agreed. She had come with her husband, Peter, whom she'd married last November. "Out of all of us, you've the sweetest temperament."

"Maybe I am coming down with something," she mumbled. She felt guilty. Henry was a *gut* man, a kind man, and once again she'd behaved badly toward him. *Again.* But how could she apologize when just the thought made her insides churn with nervous apprehension?

"You'd better make sure you get enough rest, *dochter.* I know that you didn't sleep well last night. I heard you get up for a while before you went back to bed. Why can't you sleep?"

Leah shrugged. "I felt restless, so I went down and drank some hot milk." But she knew she'd gotten very little sleep since the day she'd found shelter with Henry in the store. Since then, she was unable to forget being the focus of his intense blue eyes.

"The men have their food," Ellie said. "Let's get ours."

As the Stoltzfus women went for their meal, Leah shot a glance toward Henry and her cousins' table. A frisson of sensation rippled down her spine as she caught Henry gazing at her with an odd look in his eyes. She stared back for a long moment and tried not to think about how handsome he was or that if circumstances had been different, she would have longed for his attention. She turned away deliberately, slowly, and followed her sisters to the food tables, pretending she didn't care that he was watching her. Inside she felt a jumble of nerves, but she wasn't about to let the man see how much he rattled her.

A short time after she finished eating her lunch,

Leah had risen to help clean up when she caught sight of Henry's approach, his gaze focused on her. She stiffened even while her heart fluttered in appreciation of how handsome he was.

"Leah," he greeted softly. "May I have a word?"

"I'm cleaning up."

"I'll take care of this," Ellie offered as she grabbed the plates Leah held. She hurried away before Leah could object.

Leah shifted uncomfortably as she watched her sister stride away. She arched an eyebrow as she turned toward Henry. "Do you need me for something?"

His lips curved in a smile that stole her breath. "It's not what I need. It's about what I may be able to do for you." He paused. "Walk with me?" When she hesitated, he added softly, *"Please?"*

When he asked so nicely, how could she resist him? She nodded and fell into step beside him. Thoughts of an apology hovered in her mind.

They started toward the fields beyond the barn. Leah didn't look back, afraid to discover that others might be watching them. She experienced a tingling at her nape as they strolled some distance away from the gathering. She stopped, unwilling to go any farther.

"What do you want, Henry?"

He halted and turned her to face him. "I want to help you with your craft shop."

She gasped. "What? Who told you about it?"

"Isaac," he said calmly. "One of your sisters told him."

A ball of hurt fisted inside her chest. *"Ellie."*

Henry nodded. "Don't be angry with either one of them. It came out accidentally when Isaac and Ellie were talking. Isaac mentioned it because he thought I could help you. I know what it takes to run a store—about inventory, purchasing, merchandise displays, bookkeeping…"

Leah knew she should be angry, but for some reason something in Henry's expression softened something inside of her. "I'm not ready to open a store just yet."

"Will you think about it when you do? Me helping you?"

"That's nice of you, Henry, but—"

"You don't trust me enough."

Leah shook her head because, for some reason, she trusted him in this. "'Tis not that. I don't have enough capital to look for a place yet."

"I understand." But something in his blue eyes had dimmed. He turned as if to head back toward the main yard.

She felt the uncontrollable urge to stop him. She grabbed his arm to halt him. "I'm telling the truth, Henry. I'll be happy to accept your help when the time is right."

Henry grinned, and Leah reeled back under the bright warmth in his eyes. "*Gut.* I'll be pleased to help you. And if you need assistance looking for a place when the time is right, I'm your man."

Leah felt her face heat. *I'm your man.* She had a sudden mental image of him working with her, smiling at her, making her feel special. She glanced away. "We should get back." She started to walk and he fell into step with her.

"Danki," he murmured as they entered the barnyard.

She met his gaze. "For what?"

"For trusting me enough to accept my help," he whispered. Then, as if he'd sensed her unease, he left her, and she watched as he hurried toward the dessert table.

Shaken, Leah knew a strange yearning in her heart, one she didn't recognize. Still, she managed a smile as she rejoined her sisters where they sat drinking iced tea and sharing desserts.

Chapter Three

Monday morning Leah exited the house in good spirits. Ellie had been hired to houseclean for a new client who owned a huge five-bedroom residence. Because of the amount of work involved, her sister had requested her help. Leah was more than willing to work with Ellie. She'd put away the money for her shop. Since turning eighteen, she was allowed to keep all of her work earnings. Which was why she made it a point to help her parents as much as she could around the house and farm. It was her turn to feed the animals this morning, and she was happy to do it.

Her thoughts on the day ahead, she descended the porch steps and started forward, then halted abruptly. Her heart began to hammer hard as she stared at the man who stood several feet from her. "What are you doing here, Henry?"

He approached, and as he drew closer, she backed away until she was up against the bottom rung of the stairs. "Aren't you happy to see me?" A tiny smile curved up the corners of his mouth.

She sniffed, determined to keep him from realizing that she *was* glad to see him. "What do you think?"

His smile disappeared. "Contrary to what you might believe, I'm not stalking you."

She blushed. "I didn't say you were."

He folded his arms as he studied her. He wore a green shirt, navy tri-blend pants with black suspenders. A black-banded straw hat rested on his head, but he'd tipped back the wide brim. Beneath it, his sky blue eyes looked sapphire. "I'm here to help your father."

Leah blinked, tried to stay calm. "With what?"

Henry sighed heavily. "He wants to install a cabinet in one section of the barn to store things."

She gazed at him with suspicion. "My cousin invited you to Visiting Day, where my father just happened to ask you to install a cabinet for him, and all within four days of Friday's thunderstorm?"

He shrugged as if he didn't care whether or not she believed him. As if he was telling the truth. She frowned.

Her father came out of the house behind him. "Henry!" he exclaimed, and Leah immediately slipped past Henry before she looked back to watch the interaction between the two men. "Glad you could make it."

Leah experienced a burning in her stomach. Her *dat* seemed genuinely pleased to see him. The hot sensation intensified. Henry had told the truth. Why did she continually misjudge him?

Ashamed, she turned away, headed toward the barn to feed the animals. She started to hurry as it occurred to her that Henry and her father would be along soon. She fed all of the horses first, ensuring that each had fresh water and a bucket of feed. Later in the day, she'd return for their third feeding. Her sister Charlie would do the second one midday. She then went on to feed their dairy cows, bull, goats and sheep. She was outside with their hens and rooster when she heard voices from within the barn. When she was done throwing down chicken feed, she reluctantly returned to the outbuilding to put away the bucket. Their two cows needed to be milked, but she'd ask Charlie to do that for her. She had no desire to stay inside the barn as long as she had to share it with Henry Yoder.

Leah froze in the act of putting away the feed bucket. What was wrong with her? One minute she felt bad about the way she'd treated Henry, then in the next she was going out of her way to avoid him. She drew a cleansing breath. She wasn't going to run. She'd milk the cows before getting ready for work with Ellie. She wasn't going to let Henry's presence make her run scared.

Leah found the milk pails and went to Bessie first. Dragging over a stool, she sat down to milk her. The steady, rhythmic sound of milk against metal soothed her, and she became immersed in the farm chore. Once Bessie was milked, she moved on to Annabelle. The cow wasn't as cooperative as Bessie. The animal shifted restlessly and tried to kick her. She backed away before she was struck by the cow's hoof.

"*Nay*, you don't, you ornery critter!" She turned to get fresh hay and groaned when she saw Henry Yoder, who watched her with amusement.

"Having a bit of trouble, Leah?" he taunted, his voice deep and extremely male.

She glared at him as she lifted her chin. "Nothing I can't handle." Annabelle bumped up against her, nearly sending her sprawling. Henry's quick response to steady her made her grit her teeth.

"Need help?" he asked.

"Nay!" She was too aware of his strength as he released her.

He laughed. "Afraid I'll do it better and faster?"

"Go away," she said as she found fresh hay, which she tossed before Annabelle. The animal bent her head, content to eat. "Why are you here? I thought you were with my *vadder*." She pulled up the stool and started to milk Annabelle before she looked up at him.

He had taken off his hat and she could see the twinkle in his blue eyes. "I am," he said patiently. "He went into the house to fetch his drawings."

Leah frowned. "What drawings?" The sound of milk hitting the inside of the bucket wasn't as loud as her rapidly beating heart.

"Of the cabinet he wants me to build for him."

She paused in the act of milking. "Why would he want *you* to make him a cabinet?" Her voice sounded unnecessarily sharp. Contrite, she closed her eyes and drew a calming breath. Annabelle shifted uneasily, and Leah continued to milk her until the pail was nearly full.

"Because I like making them." He regarded her without warmth.

Leah studied him. She could see that her questioning his cabinetmaking abilities had upset him. "Have you made one before?" she said, softening her tone.

Henry nodded. "*Ja*, several."

She stifled a rude retort.

"I don't spend every minute in my parents' store," he added drily.

He'd aroused her curiosity. "Where does *Dat* want this cabinet?"

"Come with me," he invited.

Leah puckered her brow. Believing that she had little choice but to accompany him, she placed the filled milk pails into cold storage before she followed. She studied the back of his head and neck as he led the way through the barn and stopped at a familiar stall. She stared. It was the area that had housed Nell's dog, Jonas, and her cat, Maxie, then later the dog Peter Zook had given her sister Meg. Now the space was empty. *Why does* Dat *want a cabinet in here?*

She must have spoken the thought out loud. "Because he plans to get a dog," Henry said, shocking her. "With your sisters married and gone, he finds he's missing their animals. He thinks a cabinet will be a better place for dog food than on the shelf."

"*Dat* wants a dog?" she asked disbelievingly. Why hadn't her father told her?

Henry tilted his head as he regarded her. "You don't like dogs?"

She shook her head. "*Nay*—I'm mean—*ja*, I like dogs fine. I just didn't realize that my *vadder* did." Most Amish men wouldn't be willing to own a pet. Her sister Nell, who was married to a veterinarian, must have influenced her father more than she'd realized.

Before Henry could respond, her father returned, carrying a notepad. "Here you go. You can take this with you," he said as he tore off a page and handed it to Henry. He glanced at Leah briefly before turning back to the younger man.

Leah vaguely heard their discussion. She heard mention of wood and hinges and other stuff she couldn't comprehend. When the men's conversation ended, the barn became overwhelmingly quiet.

"*Dat?* You're going to get a dog?"

"I am." Arlin gazed at her with a silent look that warned her to mind her own business.

"Why didn't you tell me?" She fought back the hurt. It wasn't the first time she'd felt a little left out, set off from her family. She managed to smile. "What kind?"

Dat smiled and his demeanor changed from stern to little-boy excitement. "I don't know. What do you think?"

"I have no idea." She paused. "We could ask Nell. She'll recommend a good breed."

"I already asked her."

Nell knew. Who else? That feeling of being excluded rushed in again. She could feel Henry's gaze. Refusing to look at him, she addressed her father. "May I go with you when you pick one out?"

Her father beamed at her. "*Ja*, but I'd like to fix up the stall before I bring one home." He turned his attention to the space where the dog would be kept. "Jonas was happy here."

Leah nodded. Nell's rescue dog had been happy in these surroundings. "*Ja*, he was." She swung her gaze grudgingly toward Henry. He studied her with a thoughtful expression, and she feared that he could read the pain she'd tried to conceal while talking with her father.

"Leah!" Ellie's loud voice called from out in the yard.

"I've got to go," she said and spun around. She ran a few yards before she stopped. "See you later, *Dat*. Henry, you do a *gut* job with the cabinet, *ja*?" She softened the request with a slight curve of her lips.

Pleasure transformed Henry's features. "I will," he promised.

Leah trusted that he would. The warmth in his penetrating gaze had her scrambling to escape. She didn't want to feel anything for Henry Yoder—even the littlest, tiniest bit of warmth that settled within her chest and reached out in an unsuccessful attempt to capture her heart.

Henry watched Leah leave before turning back to Arlin. "She seems surprised that you want a dog."

Arlin had been studying his daughter as she left. He turned his focus on Henry. "She doesn't mind, though. All my *dechter* are animal lovers."

After a nod, Henry quietly studied the paper in his hands. "This looks simple enough. You want me to take down the shelf and put up a plain cabinet."

"I thought we could leave the shelf and install the cabinet to the left of it," the man said.

Henry eyed the wall space. "That would work. The dimensions for the cabinet are small."

The older man inclined his head. "Big enough, though. I'm getting a dog, not a herd of goats." He chuckled. "The two goats we have cause enough damage."

Henry didn't join in. He kept remembering the look of pain on Leah's face as she'd learned that her father hadn't bothered to include her in his plans. "When do you need this?"

"When can you get it done?"

He thought for a moment. His father was being discharged from the hospital that afternoon. He'd work in the store but figured his mother would want to spend time there. "I can have it done before Thursday."

Arlin looked surprised. *"Gut, gut."* The man headed toward the door and Henry fell into step beside him. "I was glad to see you back on Sunday." He hesitated. "I would have liked to see your *mam* and *dat*."

"*Dat's* been in the hospital. *Mam* has been spending all of her time there." Henry became quiet. "I've been running the store. My *vadder* will be released today. Maybe in a couple of weeks, they'll be able to come."

The older man regarded him with concern. "I didn't know about your *dat*." Arlin was too polite to ask, but Henry could see his curiosity.

"He had a heart attack, but his doctor says that there's no permanent damage."

"A wake-up call," Arlin said as they stepped out of the barn.

"Ja." He saw Ellie and Leah inside the buggy as Ellie steered the horse to head toward the street. He couldn't tear his attention away from the taller of the two blonde women who sat on the vehicle's passenger side.

"She can be stubborn," the man next to him murmured, catching Henry off guard. "Just like her mother."

Henry's gaze focused on Leah's father. "Who?" he asked, but he knew.

"Leah." The corners of his mouth bowed upward. "She's the sweetest and kindest of all of my *dechter*, but she can also be the most hardheaded."

"I've never known Missy to be hardheaded." Henry noted a strange look enter the man's expression and saw him stiffen.

"Leah hasn't welcomed you back to our church community, has she?" When Henry was too stunned to answer, the man continued, "Don't let it bother you. She'll get used to you soon enough."

"You think so?"

Arlin nodded. "*Ja.* 'Tis Leah. She's different than the others. I've never known her to be upset with anyone for long."

Henry took comfort from her father's belief that sooner or later Leah would accept him for the changed adult man that he'd become—and forget his foolish teenage mistakes.

His father was released from the hospital late Monday afternoon. Henry had worked on the cabinet an hour or two after the store closed. He stopped when his *dat* got home since he wanted to spend time with him and to assure his parents that the store had run smoothly with a steady flow of customers in their absence.

Henry got up extra early Tuesday morning and finished the cabinet. He had time to make a quick run to Arlin's to install it. While he drove his market wagon to the residence, he hoped to see Leah again. His heart raced at the prospect. As he pulled his vehicle into the driveway and parked near the barn, he caught a glimpse of the woman ever present in his thoughts at the clothesline, taking down laundry. She must have heard him arrive for she turned and glowered at him.

He climbed down from the wagon and reached into the back to retrieve the cabinet. He didn't realize that Leah had left the clothesline to approach until she stood within several feet of him. She watched silently as he carried the cabinet inside the barn. Henry set it in the designated stall, then left to get his tools. He accidently bumped into Leah as she entered the barn. Instinctively, he reached out to steady her.

"Careful," he murmured. She smelled like vanilla and honey, a fragrance that would forever make him think of her. *Her soap?*

He saw her throat move as she swallowed when she stepped away. "You've finished it already?" She seemed skeptical.

"Ja," he replied. "'Tis a simple design. *Gut* enough for a barn stall."

Her brow knit with confusion. "Where are you going?"

He hid his pleasure. It was as if she was afraid that he'd leave. "To get my tools." When red stained her cheeks, he realized that he'd guessed correctly. Hiding his joy, he swept past her on his way back to his wagon, where he retrieved everything he'd need for installation, including the cabinet doors, which he'd left off to make it easier for him to carry the unit. Leah hadn't moved from where he'd left her. He didn't say a word as he walked past her and into the stall.

Ignoring her, he pulled out his tape measure to gauge the distance between the small shelf to the wall corner. He'd crafted the cabinet to the right measurement. Feeling pleased, he placed two screws between his lips before he lifted the cabinet to where he wanted to secure it. Henry pulled his carpenter's pencil from behind his ear and marked within the predrilled holes before setting the unit down again. He grabbed his battery-operated screwdriver, picked up the cabinet, then screwed it into place. Once secure, he wordlessly reached for a door, which he installed before he secured the second one. When he was finished, he turned. Leah stood behind him, examining his work. She jumped back, startled as she met his gaze. He didn't say a word as he picked up his tools and headed outside.

"It looks *gut*," Leah said grudgingly as she followed him out of the barn.

He met her gaze to see if she was mocking him. She wasn't. She seemed genuinely impressed by what he'd done in so short a time. Her approval spiked his pleasure of standing in her company. "Basic and solid."

"You finished it," she said. "But it's not one that belongs in a kitchen. I think it's exactly what *Dat* had in mind."

"I just made it to look like your *vadder's* drawings."

She nodded. Her expression wasn't bitter or condemning. Henry felt his heart open like a blossom in the sun. He gazed at her a long time, then dragged his eyes away. He'd made some progress with Leah and he didn't want to press his luck. He climbed onto the wagon seat. "Show it to your *vadder* when he gets home, *ja*?"

"I will," she said.

"Take care, Leah." He turned the horse-drawn vehicle toward the main road. He flicked the leathers and his mare started forward when he heard her shout.

"Henry!"

He immediately drew in the reins to halt his horse.

She walked to his vehicle and gazed up at him. "I've decided… I'd like you to teach me about storekeeping."

He blinked, pleased. "You do?" When she nodded, he felt his heart rate accelerate. "*Gut.* There's a lot I can show you." He smiled. "Do you have a name for your shop?"

She shook her head. "I don't have a name because I don't have one yet."

"Think about a name. It will help you as you reach for your goal."

He heard her release a sharp breath. "I'll do that." She grew quiet. "I should go," she said. "I'll see you later, Henry."

"I want to know the name of your shop the next time I see you." His lips curved. "We can talk about your plans then."

"Sunday?" she asked, almost like an invitation.

He nodded. "I'll see you then."

When she beamed at him, he left with the mental image of her lovely face turned toward him, her gaze without censure. It wasn't forgiveness or friendship he'd seen in her blue eyes, but it was a start. He grinned. He couldn't wait to see her again. She'd become important to him. He attributed his anticipation to his interest in her as a woman and a prospective friend.

Leah groaned as Henry pulled his buggy onto the main road. What had she done? She'd been impressed by the cabinet he'd made, but was that any reason to ask the man if he was coming to their church service? Like she *wanted* him there?

She couldn't believe she'd been so impulsive. Why had she accepted his offer of assistance? Henry Yoder was trouble and she certainly didn't want or need it in her life. She had enough to contend with. Working with Ellie yesterday had been wonderful. They'd earned a great deal of money, and Leah was able to put a substantial amount away for her shop.

"I can do this. It will be business only," she murmured as she took down the laundry.

She exhaled with relief. She'd be polite, businesslike,

but she wouldn't give him any special attention. She would express her gratitude, of course. He was offering her his time, and she was thankful. A working relationship with him was nothing to be concerned about.

Her heart skipped a beat as she recalled his smile, the way the sunlight had reflected on the tiny golden streaks in his dark hair. Leah closed her eyes in shock. She was attracted to Henry Yoder. As long as she kept her distance emotionally from him, she would be fine.

"I'll not lose my heart to him," she whispered. And she found herself relaxing. She just had to remember that this was Henry Yoder, and she was interested only in opening a craft store.

She'd unpinned the last garment from the clothesline and headed back to the house. She smiled when she spied her father as he came home from a day spent with Horseshoe Joe Zook, Meg's father-in-law. *Dat* had been helping Joe with a home project. What, Leah had no idea.

"Dat," she greeted. "Henry was here. He installed the cabinet you ordered."

Her father looked surprised. "Already?"

She bobbed her head.

"How does it look?"

"*Gut.* 'Tis perfect for the barn."

He appeared pleased. "Come to take a look with me?"

Leah beamed. "*Ja.* Just let me put this inside," she said as she held up the laundry basket.

A few minutes later she followed her father into the stall. He went straight over to inspect the cabinet. She waited with rapid heartbeat for his reaction. Why, she didn't know. Certainly it wasn't because she worried that he wouldn't be pleased with Henry's work.

"Dat?" she murmured as he opened and closed the cabinet doors several times while he inspected every inch of the unit.

He closed the doors one last time, then turned to her—and smiled. *"Wunderbor,"* he pronounced. "When can you come with me to Nell's to look at some puppies?"

Leah grinned. "Tonight? After supper?" she suggested.

"After supper," her father agreed, then they headed toward to the house to see how long it would be before dinner.

She was excited about having a pet. Her spirits rose. It wasn't because her *dat* was pleased with Henry's cabinetwork, she thought. Or was it?

A mental image of Henry rose in her mind, making her uncomfortable. She wasn't attracted to him. She didn't like him. She sighed. His kindness stirred up feelings that she could control because they weren't real. *They can't be real.*

Leah became to wonder if she should forget about accepting Henry's offer to help. Surely, she could learn about storekeeping on her own. It would be much safer that way.

Chapter Four

Leah couldn't get Henry's offer of assistance out of her thoughts. Ever since she'd accepted it yesterday, she'd vacillated between telling him she'd changed her mind and letting her acceptance stand.

She was alone in the kitchen doing the breakfast dishes. Her mother was cleaning the upstairs and her father was out delivering his newly built wooden birdhouses to several shops in the Lancaster area. Ellie was on a housecleaning job and she wasn't sure where Charlie was, but it had to be elsewhere since Leah could always tell when her youngest sister was home. The girl was a whirlwind of activity and conversation one couldn't ignore.

She washed the dishes, then picked up one from the drain rack to dry with a clean tea towel. She gazed out the window as she dried each cup and dish and found comfort in the simple chore.

"Leah!" her mother called from upstairs. "Would you please take care of the animals?"

"Ja, Mam!" she called back.

Mam entered the kitchen a minute later as Leah put

away the last dish. "I sent Charlie to Katie's with our quilt squares."

"Too quiet for her to be here." Leah grinned. *Endie* Katie hosted their monthly quilting bee, and whenever there was a new quilt to be made, her aunt would sew the squares together, then ready the quilt to be hand stitched by the women who attended the gathering. Thoughts of quilts brought her right back to Henry, as anything crafty made her yearn to get her shop up and running. And Henry was going to help her.

Henry hadn't mentioned a time for them to meet. If he'd heard him right, she'd see him at church services. But what if he had changed his mind about teaching her? *I hope not.* She felt a painful wrenching in her midsection. Leah knew at that moment that she would let her acceptance of his offer stand. She prayed that he'd ready to teach her soon.

She hung up the dish towel. "You done upstairs?" she asked her mother as she headed toward the back door.

"*Nay.* I need to strip and wash the bedsheets."

"I can help with those," Leah offered.

But her mother shook her head. "No need. It won't take me long."

"I'll head out to the barn then. Call me if you change your mind."

Her mother's expression was warm and loving. "You're a *gut dochter*, Leah."

"You say that to all your *dechter*."

Mam laughed. "And each of you is special in your own way," she said as she headed toward the stairs.

With a smile lingering on her lips, Leah crossed the yard and entered the barn. The aroma of animal dung and straw hit her as she made her way toward the goats.

It was a scent that she was used to so she didn't mind. In fact, she found the familiarity of it soothing. The goats gravitated to her when they saw her.

"*Hallo* there, little ones. Hungry?" She opened the rear door of the barn that led to the pasture. Then she returned to release the latch on the goat stall and herded them outside. "Some lovely fresh grass for you to enjoy," she said fondly.

The small animals were quick to frolic about before stopping to graze. Leah filled the water trough near the fence, then returned to the barn to feed the horses before releasing them into the pasture with the goats. She fed the chickens, then went inside to feed their cows, and after that, she took care of their bull, Mortimer, and released him into a separate fenced area.

When all of the animals had been seen to, Leah meandered down the aisle to where their puppy would live once he was old enough to be parted from his mother. Her gaze settled on the cabinet Henry had crafted that hung on the far wall. She sighed. It looked good and it would work well for storage. She glanced down to where Nell's and then Meg's dogs had slept, saw matted bedding and frowned. Last evening when she'd come into the barn, she'd put down the fresh straw, but this morning it looked as if someone had lain there.

Her lips curved. Charlie. No doubt her sister had escaped here for a few moments to enjoy some privacy. Charlie was as excited as *Dat* about having a new pet. She could picture her little sister as Charlie lay back and stared at the barn rafters while she chewed on or fingered a piece of straw. Without thought, Leah retrieved a rake to fluff up the bedding before she put it away.

She wondered if her mother needed anything from the store. *Yoder's General Store.*

She exited the barn and stopped abruptly to avoid colliding into a solid male form. "Henry!" She gasped.

If he'd been startled by their near collision, Henry didn't show it. His mouth curved up slowly. His blue eyes warmed. "Leah, just the person I want to see."

She felt a fluttering in her chest. "I didn't expect you to visit today."

"I thought I'd stop by to see when you wanted to start storekeeping lessons. Didn't want to wait until Sunday." He shoved his straw hat back on his head, exposing more of his dark hair.

She felt the shock of looking closely into his blue eyes. Leah swallowed hard. The man was far too good-looking for her peace of mind. "I don't know. When's a *gut* time for you?"

"Tomorrow? Nine o'clock? *Mam's* working the store today." He smiled. "She brought my *vadder* with her. I'll be handling the store tomorrow. In between customers, I can show you our store account books. Go over some things that may help you." He gazed at her steadily as if trying to read her thoughts.

Tomorrow? She shifted as she found it difficult to breathe. "Can we go outside?" she asked huskily. It was strange standing in the door of the barn and she desperately needed the fresh air.

He nodded, stepped aside and gestured for her to precede him. Once they were both outside, he fell into step with her. Without a word, they headed toward the back of the property, around the fenced area and into the farm field, away from the road and the prying eyes of anyone who might drive by and see them together.

If he wondered why she chose this direction, Henry didn't mention it. Leah chanced a look at him and encountered the direct impact of his gaze. Her heart thumped hard. Twice. Three times. She glanced away. "I don't want you to feel obligated to do this for me. I know you sell crafts in your store and…"

He halted and she jolted when he placed a gentle hand on her shoulder. "Leah, I want to help you. As for the crafts in our store? They don't sell well there, because our focus is food and supplies and our customers are mostly members of our Amish community. But a craft shop like the one you want to open? It will draw business from two directions—from community members who will want you to sell their items to English residents of Happiness and to tourists who are visiting the area." He seemed taken back as he noted where he'd placed his hand. He quickly released her. "We need a craft store. Your shop will do well, I'm sure of it."

The earnestness in his expression moved her. "I hope you're right," she whispered. She continued to walk. She knew she should get back to the house, but for some reason she wanted to prolong her time with him. Considering how she'd felt about him before the day she'd taken refuge from the storm, she found her change of heart somewhat disturbing, as well as exciting. She still wasn't sure just how much she should trust him. *As long as I consider him a teacher and nothing more, there is no cause for me to worry.*

They walked until they reached the road that bordered the rear of the property. "This land is your *vadder's*?" Henry asked.

Leah nodded. "It used to belong to Aaron Troyer, but he decided to move closer to Lancaster City, where he runs his buggy-ride business. *Dat* bought it to add to the farm."

He nodded as if he knew of Aaron's business. "He does well with tourists."

"*Ja*, and he enjoys it. His sister, Martha, helps him." Leah frowned. "Sometimes I wonder…" She stopped as she realized that she shouldn't voice her thoughts, that she often wondered if Aaron wasn't lonely without a wife or family. He was in his late twenties or early thirties. He was a nice man, although she hadn't spent a lot of time in his company. She had no idea why she was now thinking of his personal business.

"You wonder what?" Henry stopped and faced her.

Leah shook her head. "'Tis nothing." She smiled up at him. "And none of my business." He frowned. She was grateful that he didn't push. "We should head back."

She turned and started forward. He halted her with a touch on her arm. She inhaled sharply as she gazed at him. "Is something wrong?"

He didn't say a word as he continued to study her. His perusal seemed almost like a caress, but that was only her imagination. There was nothing but polite concern in his expression. "What's bothering you?"

She tilted her head as she furrowed her brow. "Why do you ask?"

Henry gazed at the woman before him, feeling concern. He couldn't tell what she was thinking. He had a feeling that she was struggling with something, and all he wanted to do was help. He just hoped that the something wasn't *him*. "You still want me to teach you?"

Her gaze met his, then skittered away. "*Ja*, I can learn a lot from you."

"But?" he asked as his stomach burned. What if she'd changed her mind? He honestly wanted to help and spend time with her.

She met his regard head-on. "I just wonder if 'tis a *gut* idea. I feel like I'm taking advantage."

Stunned by her answer, he shook his head. "*Nay.* You forget this was *my* idea."

Leah seemed afraid to believe him. "Are you sure?"

His lips curved from a smile into a full-out grin. "Positive. If you'd like, you can help with customers."

He saw her relax and felt gratified. *"Danki,"* she murmured.

"I'm more than happy to help, Leah."

As they headed back toward the house, Henry felt the tension ease between them. He and Leah Stoltzfus would be spending a lot of time together. He hoped that she'd come to accept the man he'd become. That his mistake was a while ago should have made things easier for them, but he realized that when it came to family, it wasn't easier to forgive and forget despite the teachings of the Amish faith.

Leah accompanied him to his buggy. "I'll see you tomorrow," she said.

She stepped back to allow him room to climb into his vehicle. Her mother exited the house and approached.

"Who'll be hosting church service next?" he asked, figuring she would know. He'd forgotten to ask Isaac when he'd seen him last.

"We are," Missy said as she drew near. "The Kings were to host, but there's been a family emergency."

Henry frowned. "I hope it's nothing serious."

"I don't know. Mae and Amos had to leave for Ohio. I believe Mae's brother is ill."

"I'll keep everyone in my prayers," he said.

Missy nodded as if she approved. Henry glanced at Leah. "See you soon." He then waved at the two women as he steered his horse back to the road. He didn't look back until he reached the street. He wasn't surprised that the women had gone inside the house, although he realized how much he'd hoped that Leah would linger outside until he left.

As he headed back to the family store, he looked forward to the next morning. He was eager to show Leah how they kept their books. He hadn't mentioned the lessons to his parents, but he didn't see why they would think them a problem. He would show Leah a ledger page and explain about accounting columns and how to keep track of inventory, as well as accounts receivable and payable.

He was also eager for Sunday since it was to be held at the Arlin Stoltzfus farm. It would be wonderful seeing more of Leah's home and how she and her family related to each other. Henry was the youngest of three siblings. His eldest brother had chosen to leave the Amish life. His parents were upset by his choice, not because he'd done anything wrong by leaving when he had. He hadn't joined the church, so he was free to live an English life if he chose. His father and mother were upset because David had moved away and hadn't been home to visit in years and the last letter they'd received had been over ten months ago. Henry wondered how his older brother was faring. There were many years between them, so it seemed as if they'd grown up in different families. His sister, Ruth, was married and living in Ohio. Henry couldn't recall the last time he'd seen her. He had written to her recently to let her know about their father's hospital stay. If Ruth didn't come after receiving the news, then he didn't know how to convince her that it was well past the time for her to visit.

He thought of Leah, who was constantly in his thoughts. He was encouraged that she trusted him enough to allow him to help. He grinned as he flicked his horse's leathers and urged the animal into a fast trot toward home.

When he arrived, he went to the store first to check on his parents. Earlier, he'd talked with them about returning to their former community. They'd said they would think about it, and he'd had the impression that they were going to agree. He needed to make sure that they were still willing to go. If so, he could help his mother prepare her contribution to the midday meal that the church members enjoyed after service was finished.

He opened the door to the shop and stepped inside. It was bright outside and it took a minute for his eyes to adjust to the change in light. *"Mam?"*

"Henry!" she exclaimed as she caught sight of him. "I thought you were spending the day with Isaac."

"I did for a while, but he had work to finish and I do, too. I stopped by the Stoltzfuses. Do you remember the cabinet I was building? It was for Arlin. He wanted it for his barn."

His mother smiled but seemed preoccupied.

"Where's *Dat*? Isn't he here?"

"*Nay*, he was feeling tired so I sent him home to rest."

"*Mam*, do you think he's ill?"

"I don't know, but I think I'll ask to move up his doctor's appointment."

Henry thought his mother's decision wise. "Would

you like me to check on him? Or I can stay here if you'd like to go back to the house yourself."

"Would you go? I'd go myself but I'm expecting Alta Hershberger."

Alta Hershberger was the local busybody from their former Amish church community.

"I'll let you know if anything is wrong," he assured her. "I won't bother him if he's sleeping. He may be tired because of his medication."

"I hope that's all it is," his *mam* said with a look of worry.

Henry left the store and parked close to the house barnyard. *"Dat?"* he called not too loudly as he entered. If his father was awake, he'd be able to hear his call. If not, then his *dat* was probably asleep.

When there was no answer, he walked through the house to check each room until he found his father in the bedroom. He approached silently and was glad to see his *dat's* even and easy breathing as his parent slept. He left as quietly as he'd come and went into the kitchen for a glass of iced tea and a bite to eat. He'd bring his mother lunch while assuring her that *Dat* was resting comfortably. He made two ham-and-cheese sandwiches, then he headed back to the store down the lane from the house.

When he got back, he saw Alta Hershberger in conversation with his mother. He entered and greeted Alta with a smile. The woman looked at him speculatively, acknowledged his greeting, then abruptly turned back to his mother. He met his *mam's* gaze briefly, and the look in her eyes apologized for Alta's behavior. Henry went quietly into the back room where they often ate midday meals while at work. He set the sandwiches on the table, then went out front to grab two bottles of iced tea from the refrigerated display case. With a nod in Alta's direction, he returned to the back and waited for his mother.

He didn't have to wait too long. His mother entered moments later, saw the tea and sandwiches on the table and smiled. "How thoughtful!"

Henry's mouth curved. "I thought you might be hungry."

"I am." She pulled out a chair and sat. "I'm sorry about Alta."

"There's no need to apologize. Alta is Alta. She is who she is."

"She has a good heart."

He nodded. "But most of the time she hides it." He chuckled. "She doesn't bother me." He took a bite of his sandwich and watched his *mam* do the same. He felt happy when he saw his *mam's* enjoyment of the simple meal. "*Dat's* sleeping."

His mother frowned as she set down the sandwich. "I'm worried about him."

"He seems to be resting comfortably."

"But the doctor said there was no permanent damage to his heart. Why is he so tired?"

He pushed his mother's bottle of tea closer to her. "I don't know, but I agree that he should see the doctor." He thought of Sunday service and longed for assurances that his parents would be attending. "*Mam*, you'll come to church services at Arlin's *haus*, *ja*?"

She furrowed her brow. "I want to."

"Everyone has been asking after you." He reached for her hand. "*Mam*, please don't let my past mistakes keep you from your friends. I know you've made new ones in the new church district, but this community—

the Lapps, Stoltzfuses, Kings and others—miss you. They want to see you."

Her blue eyes glistened. "They do?"

"*Mam*, I know Alta can be difficult," he began.

She laughed. "As you said, Alta is Alta. She doesn't bother me."

"Then will you and *Dat* come?"

His mother nodded. "We'll be there."

He relaxed and smiled. *"Gut."* He took a bite of his sandwich, chewed and swallowed. "I thought I'd work in the store tomorrow so you'll be able to spend time with *Dat* and keep an eye on him."

Mam looked relieved. "That's a fine idea. *Danki.*"

Henry grinned. "You're welcome." He picked up his iced tea and sipped. "I figured I'd help Isaac with the bench wagon Saturday."

"Tell him I said *hallo*."

Henry beamed at her. "I will." He suddenly had a lot to look forward to, starting with Leah's first storekeeping lesson tomorrow, then spending time helping Isaac on the Stoltzfus property on Saturday and returning again on Sunday for church services. He'd get to see Leah on three, maybe even four, occasions if he could convince her to return for lesson two on Friday, he thought with a rush of pleasure.

He couldn't wait.

Chapter Five

Leah woke up Thursday morning, eager to learn more about storekeeping from Henry. Her sister Ellie had asked her to help with a job late yesterday afternoon, and she'd been pleased for the work, for she had more earnings to add to her savings. She planned to accept any work Ellie offered her from now on while learning what she could whenever Henry was available to teach her. A general store wasn't the same as a craft shop, but surely the bookkeeping and ordering of merchandise would be similar. She showered, then donned a light purple dress with black apron and white prayer *kapp* over her hair. Figuring that she'd be on her feet helping him with customers, she put on comfortable black shoes that allowed her to stand for long periods of time.

"Morning, Leah," her mother greeted as Leah entered the kitchen for breakfast.

"*Gut* mornin', *Mam*. I'll plan to pick up a few things at Yoder's store this morning. Do you need anything?"

"That's nice of you, Leah." *Mam* turned and reached for a sheet of paper on the kitchen countertop. "I already have a list."

She took and studied it. She saw several items that made her wonder how soon her mother might want them. "*Mam*, I may stay awhile. Do you need these right away?"

"Whenever you get home will be fine, Leah. I'm off to help Josie Mast with her baking. Now that Ellen is married and out of the house, Josie feels that she needs someone to teach her to bake a pie without making a mess of it."

Leah chuckled. "I know she has trouble. Ellen confided in me about it. Josie is a fine cook, just not a *gut* baker." She grabbed a muffin from a plate, made a cup of tea and then sat down to enjoy both. "Where's Charlie?" she asked.

"Charlotte Peachy has asked her to help with the children today. She left about five minutes before you came down."

"The Peachy residence, eh?" She grinned at her mother. "I'm surprised she agreed to go. She's not overly fond of Nate."

Mam gave her a slow smile. "He's not going to be there."

"No wonder she agreed," Leah murmured.

It didn't take her long to eat her muffin and finish her tea. She rose and brought her dishes to the sink, where she washed and dried them before putting them away.

"Are you sure you've eaten enough?" her mother asked.

"I'll be fine. If I get hungry, I can always buy something to munch on at the store."

Mam nodded. "I'll see you later then. Give Harry and Margaret my best. And Henry, too."

The mention of Henry's name made her blush. "I

will." She felt suddenly nervous about the upcoming lesson.

Less than a half hour later, Leah steered her horse-drawn buggy into the parking area near Yoder's General Store. She got out of the vehicle, tied up her horse and went to the front store entrance. The door was unlocked and opened easily. "Henry?" she called.

He came out from the back, looking pleased to see her. He looked handsome in a green shirt and blue tri-blend pants held up with black suspenders. She admired his dark hair, for he always took off his hat inside.

"You came," he said as if he hadn't been sure she'd actually show. "Come around to the back." He jerked his head toward the rooms beyond the merchandise area.

Breath hitching, she followed him around the counter to the room where she and Henry had taken shelter during that terrible spring thunderstorm.

He led the way into another room that she hadn't noticed before. There was a desk and a large book, opened, with pages of columns and rows filled with figures and descriptions. A chair sat behind the desk, and she watched as Henry pulled another one next to it.

"I thought we'd start with bookkeeping," he said. His blue eyes regarded her with warmth. "'Tis always *gut* for a store owner to know how to manage her accounts." He pulled the chair out from under the desk. "Sit here."

Trying to calm the butterflies in her stomach, she sat where instructed. Henry shifted the other chair so that he could sit close to her. She immediately became aware of his clean masculine scent. He smelled of soap and cinnamon. As he sat beside her, she asked, "Are you baking cinnamon buns?"

He grinned, and she felt his good humor with a tingling

right down to her toes. "*Mam* made them this morning. I've brought some down for us. Want one?"

She felt her face heat. "*Ja*, please."

Henry rose and left the room. He returned moments later with two cups of hot tea and a plate with four large cinnamon rolls. "Here you go."

"You made me tea," she said breathlessly.

"You like tea with two sugars but no milk," he replied as if proud that he'd remembered.

Startled that he knew, she accepted the cup with a nod of thanks. "You made the tea here?"

"I did." He shoved the plate of cinnamon rolls toward her. "Eat up. We've got a lot to cover, so you'd better enjoy them before we get busy."

Henry watched with enjoyment as Leah sipped at her tea between bites of cinnamon roll. He was glad she was here. He knew he needed to be careful with her. He didn't want to scare her off. She didn't trust him completely, and he didn't blame her. Still, it was a comfortable silence as they finished their breakfast. When they were done, he pulled the ledger book closer to her and began to explain the system of logging income and expenses.

"What is this?" she asked, pointing to a column that listed merchandise ordered from an out-of-state company.

"We order some of our stock locally and from Ohio, Indiana and West Virginia. Once we place an order, we write the quantity of items requested in this column, the cost in this column, and see this? This is where we list the date of the order. We also keep track of the day the items arrived, whether we received everything we requested and the date we paid the invoice. Lastly, we keep track of how many we sell so that we can figure out when to place the next order."

Leah studied the ledger page carefully. "Makes sense." She glanced toward him just as he leaned closer, and he found their faces close enough for him to see the deep blue flecks in her eyes. She had beautiful fair skin and a lovely pert nose. He saw her swallow thickly before she said, "I'll have to figure out how to stock my store. I hope to sell crafts from the women in our church community on consignment, but I also want to sell sewing supplies and other craft items that will appeal to tourists in our area." Her lips were pink and he stared at them before he quickly sat back and looked away.

"That's a sound idea." He rose, needing to put some distance between them before he said or did anything to upset her, which he'd immediately regret. He crossed the room, then faced her. "Have you given any thought to a name for your shop?"

She blinked. "I've had a few ideas, but they seem silly."

Bracing himself with his palms flat against the wall behind him, Henry leaned back and studied her. "Tell me."

"Second Sister's Crafts."

He smiled as he gazed at her. "I like it."

"Or Happiness Quilt and Craft Supplies."

"I like that one, too." He loved looking at her. Their eyes caught and held, and he fought the urge to look away. From a distance, he felt more in control of his emotions. Leah Stoltzfus was getting to him in a way he'd never expected. He longed for more than friendship from her. But that was impossible. The goal was to get her to forgive him and be his friend. He'd be polite and helpful, and make sure she couldn't read his thoughts—or his attraction to her. The room grew silent. Henry felt a rising tension. "Would you like more tea?" he asked, pushing himself from the wall.

She looked down briefly at her cup and nodded. "That would nice."

He stared at her intently a moment, unable to look away from her beautiful eyes and face, until he realized he'd made her uncomfortable. "I'll be right back," he murmured before heading into the front room. He checked the contents of the teakettle and realized there was enough water to heat back up. He set it on the propane single-burner unit they kept on the table behind the counter and turned it on. Henry looked down and saw that they needed more tea, so he went down one of the store aisles and grabbed a box of tea bags. The store entrance door opened just as he stepped behind the counter. He glanced back and felt a moment's dread when he realized that it was Alta Hershberger, the community busybody, who'd entered.

Hoping to alert Leah of potential trouble, he moved close toward the opening to the back room. "*Gut* morning, Alta!" he said loudly enough for Leah to hear. "What can I help you with this fine day?"

"Henry." The woman narrowed her gaze as she studied him. "Have you been staying out of trouble?"

Henry stiffened but managed to smile. "*Ja*, I've learned my lesson." Some imp inside of him said, "And you?"

Alta sniffed. "As if I would do something so outrageous to be considered trouble."

He barely managed not to grit his teeth. "May I help you find something?"

Suddenly all business, she moved closer to the

counter. "I have a list," she said, shoving it in his direction.

Henry studied the paper and nearly groaned. The list looked a mile long, and it appeared that now that she saw he was here, she expected him to pull all the merchandise for her. And since some of the items sported different brands, he had a feeling that whatever one he picked for her wouldn't meet her expectations. With a sigh, he grabbed a handbasket and started down the first aisle.

The teakettle whistled, drawing Alta's attention. "You're making tea?" she asked. "*Gut.* I'd like a cup."

Fighting irritation because he was here, after all, to help their store customers, even one as contrary as Alta Hershberger, he smiled as he came around to the back of the counter where he set down the basket to prepare the woman a cup of tea. He poured water into a clean cup, added a tea bag from the box he'd taken from the shelf, then set it on the counter before her. "Sugar? Milk?"

"Sugar," she said with a raised eyebrow as she studied the tea bag. "Lots of it. This kind can be bitter."

"Ja," he agreed pleasantly as he set the sugar bowl and a clean spoon before her.

"Do you have a chair?"

"I'll get you one." Henry was eager to go into the back and see Leah in case she hadn't heard him and didn't know of Alta's presence in the store. The last thing he wanted was for the woman to find out that Leah was in the back room. He entered the room where she'd sat at the desk only to find it empty. His heart lurched and he placed a hand over his burning stomach. Leah was gone. She hadn't waited for him to return.

He grabbed the chair he'd been sitting in only moments ago and brought it out for Alta.

"Here you go."

To his shock, her expression softened and she smiled at him with approval.

The front door opened again. "*Gut* morning!" the newcomer said. Henry was stunned to Leah acting as if she'd just arrived with list in hand. "Nice day for shopping, isn't it?" Her eyes fell on Alta and Leah beamed at her. "You had the same idea as my *mudder*!" Her gaze shifted to Henry, but there was nothing in it to give away her thoughts. He couldn't help feel pleased that she hadn't left. She must have heeded his warning and found this entrance the best solution to a possible bad situation.

She approached where Henry stood and Alta was seated. "Henry, I'm sorry to bother you on a day that you're busy, but *Mam* asked that I pick up a few things for her. When you're done with Alta, do you think you could help me?"

He kept his features polite as he nodded. "It will take me a few minutes. Alta is having tea. Would you like a cup?"

"*Ja*, that would be wonderful," she said, and a quick glimmer of amusement flickered in her blue eyes. His mood lightened. "But I'll make it…if it's *oll recht*," she added.

His smile was genuine. "Feel free."

"Use lots of sugar," Alta grumbled as Leah skirted the counter to the teakettle.

"Cups are below." Henry had moved back into the first aisle where he began to assemble Alta's grocery order. He took his time, making sure he got everything on Alta's list. He questioned her on a few things, and she seemed to approve of his diligence in getting the correct items.

He no longer minded Alta's presence, because Leah had stayed and was making herself at home. Soon the older woman would finish her tea, pay for her order and leave. And Leah would still be here. *She had stayed. Thanks be to God.*

Three hours later Henry was alone in the store, cleaning the teacups left behind by Alta Hershberger and Leah. The morning—the day—hadn't turned out as he'd hoped. After he'd filled Alta's order, he'd started on Leah's but, instead of leaving as expected, Alta had stayed for another cup of tea. When he was done with Leah's order, there was nothing for her to do but leave. The woman had taken it as a given that Leah would want to continue their conversation outside. Unfortunately, Leah hadn't come back into the store, and Henry began to wonder if she'd ever return. He wanted badly to work with her and be her friend. He had to fight his rising feelings for her. There'd be only heartbreak if he gave in to them.

It was one o'clock in the afternoon. Leah and Alta had been gone for over two hours. Only two other customers had come into the shop, but, unlike, Alta they grabbed the items they wanted from the shelves without help. Henry had smiled and made polite conversation, even answering questions about his *dat's* health. Everyone was glad that his father was home and recovering, and they commended him for stepping in to keep the store running.

Henry had work to do in the back. He needed to note what had been sold in the last month and make a list of what to order. Gazing at the front door, he got an idea. He walked to the last aisle, where he grabbed a small goat's bell. Then he secured it to the inside of the entrance so that he would hear if anyone came in. After opening and shutting the door a few times, he was pleased that the bell alert would work. Then he turned with a heavy sigh toward the back room, wondering when he could approach Leah about her next lesson. He sincerely hoped that Alta's appearance hadn't convinced her that it would be wiser if she didn't come. He liked having Leah in the store with him. He liked sitting close and explaining all the columns and rows in the accounts ledger book. He prayed that this morning wouldn't be the last time that Leah allowed him to help her.

Henry got down to the business of the account books when he heard the bell on the front door, signaling someone had entered. He pushed back his chair and stood. He had started toward the store area when a figure blocked the doorway.

"I thought she'd never leave," Leah said with a smile.

He experienced a lightness that came only in her presence. "I figured you went home."

She stepped back as he continued toward the front. "I did, but only to bring *Mam's* groceries home. I'd always planned to come back." A concerned look came over her pretty features. "I'm sorry. Is this a bad time?"

He shook his head. He was happy to see her. "This is the perfect time." He grinned. "Want a soda?"

Her lips twitched. "What, no offer of tea?"

Arching an eyebrow, he asked, "Would you rather have tea?"

"*Nay*, I had enough just waiting for Alta to leave. Once I realized that she wasn't going to go without me,

I gave up and followed her outside." She reached to adjust her prayer *kapp*. "I came back as fast as I could, but Alta—she kept me outside talking for over an hour."

"*Ach nay!* I'm sorry for that."

Leah laughed. "It was fine. I didn't give her anything to natter about. She filled me in about everyone's business, then left after making sure I drove my buggy toward home. She followed me."

He reached into the store's refrigerated case for two sodas. "Cola or root beer?"

"Root beer," she said.

He opened a bottle of root beer and handed it to her. She accepted it with a nod of thanks. "I'm glad you came back."

"I'd hoped to make things easier for you," she murmured. She glanced about the store. "Can we work out here? In case someone else comes? Will you let me wait on customers? I'd like to help."

"You would?" He thought her truly an amazing woman.

"*Ja*, it will be a *gut* experience," she said. Her eyes settled on the front entrance. "I like the bell you put on the door."

"Some might think it too fancy, but I thought it necessary to know when someone comes while I'm working in the back." He grinned. "When *we're* working in the back."

"Does Alta come in often?"

"At least once a week."

"So she won't be back until next week."

"I can't guarantee it, but I don't think she will." He couldn't take his eyes off her. "What do you want to learn next?"

"Can we go back to the ledger book?"

"I'll get it," he said. "I think it's a wise idea to work out here. We can use the table behind the counter." He studied the space. "You won't be able to sit, though. Do you mind standing while we work?"

"Does a rooster crow?" she replied with laughter in her eyes and her tone.

He chuckled, delighted. "I believe it does."

"I don't mind," she assured him.

The afternoon flew by quickly for Henry as Leah listened to him explain how his mother had organized the accounts. "I made a few changes that seem to work better," he said. "Fortunately, *Mam* agrees."

When it came time for Leah to leave, Henry broached the subject of looking for a craft store location.

"I don't know," Leah hedged worriedly. "Isn't it too early to look?"

"Not if you can find a place you can afford. You said you'd been saving for years. As long as you have enough for a security deposit, if necessary, and the first two months' rent."

"But I'll need merchandise."

"You can start with the women in the community. I'm sure they have crafts they'd like to sell."

Leah looked thoughtful. "That's what I'd hoped for." She smiled. "We can go. You'll come, *ja*?"

He felt his lips curve. Considering how she'd felt about him, he felt grateful that she trusted him enough to want him to come. "I wouldn't have it any other way." He was embarrassed when she raised her eyebrows. He knew he had no right to assume that she'd want his help in this, but he really wanted to accompany her as she checked out different places to rent. "Sorry."

Her laughter rang out, surprising him. "I won't go unless you come with me, Henry. I really could use your help."

"And I honestly want to help you," he said, unable to tamp down the happiness her admission caused. He had to remind himself that this was business with her, nothing more. "When?"

"How about tomorrow morning?"

"I'll come for you," Henry suggested.

She bobbed her head. "Nine?"

"See you then," he promised.

Chapter Six

Friday morning Leah found herself alone in the house. Everyone in her family had someplace to go, including her, but it was only eight in the morning so she had time to do a few chores before Henry's arrival. Grabbing a broom and dust rag, she decided to start upstairs. It would be one less thing for her mother to do later.

The day was warm and balmy. The first thing she did was open the windows to allow in the fresh air. She checked each of the bedrooms to ensure that the beds were made. If not, then she knew that she'd have time to strip off and launder the sheets. She cleaned Ellie's room first, then moved on to Charlie's. She had already tidied her own room earlier, so after she finished with her youngest sisters' bedchambers, she entered her parents' room.

Her *mam* had already made the bed and opened the bedroom windows. Leah dusted the top of the small chest of drawers and the low wooden chest at the end of the bed. When she was done, she grabbed the broom and swept the floor, reaching under the bed for any dust that may have settled. As she pushed the corn bristles farther underneath, she felt the broom bump into something hard. She crouched down and was surprised to discover a heavy-duty cardboard box. Odd, she thought, that her mother didn't store whatever was in the box in the wooden chest at the end of their bed. She used the broom to push the box out from underneath the bed frame. Then she leaned the broom in the corner and picked up the box. Curious, she lifted the lid and looked inside.

The first thing she saw were several school papers from her and each of her sisters. She smiled, remembering when she had done hers. She'd been learning English and the teacher in Ohio had made her students write English words several times until they remembered the meanings, the spellings and the pronunciations as they said the words aloud.

She was overwhelmed with fond memories as she dug deeper into the box's contents. There was her sister Nell's birth certificate—and there was Meg's, Ellie's and Charlie's. Curious to see her own, Leah flipped through other papers until she spied hers near the bottom of the box. She pulled out the certificate and stared. It wasn't her birth certificate. It was another document with her name and her parents' names. Adoption papers. Leah gasped and felt an immediate sense of betrayal. Her parents' names were listed as the adoptive parents of a baby girl named Leah.

The words blurred as she realized what her parents had been keeping from her. She wasn't a Stoltzfus sister but some girl without a real mother and father. Her eyes overflowed with tears. Somewhere in the back of her mind she acknowledged that Arlin and Missy Stoltzfus had been good to her, that they must care for her a great deal if they had been willing to bring her into their home. *They felt sorry for me.*

But where did she come from? How did she end up being placed with this particular family? She experienced a shaft of pain when she thought of her sisters, who weren't really her sisters.

Why, Dat*? Why,* Mam*? Why didn't you tell me?*

She wasn't a Stoltzfus daughter. She'd sometimes felt as if she didn't belong. *Not sisters*, she thought with a sob. *Not blood.* And hadn't she wondered why her parents never encouraged her to marry like they did the others?

Sobbing, she put the papers back in the order she'd found them and shoved the box back under the bed. Then she swept the rest of the floor with tears running down her face. When she was done, she put away the broom and escaped to the barn where she could cry in earnest. She didn't want any Stoltzfus family member to see her tears. She didn't know what to do. *I don't belong here. Who am I? Do I have any relatives who want to know me?*

Didn't her real mother want her? What about her father? Had he rejected her, too?

She ran through the barn, slipped out the back exit, then slid down the wall to her knees, where she continued to cry as her heart broke. She cried until there was no more tears, until she felt numb inside. Leah got up and went back into the barn. Without thought, she headed toward the front of the barn and found herself in the stall which would house the new dog. As planned, she and her father had visited Nell and James to take a look at a litter of puppies. They had picked out a cute little mixed-breed puppy, but her sister wanted to ensure that the puppy had his vaccinations before releasing him into their care. Nell had promised to bring the little dog by today. Dat *will be excited to see him!* As she entered the stall, she felt tears well up again.

Not my vadder. *Not my sister. Not my dog.*

Hugging herself with her arms, Leah slunk down to sit on the fresh bed of straw and sobbed loudly.

Henry was happy. He looked forward to spending the day with Leah. While he knew he should be careful about keeping himself emotionally protected from heartbreak, he couldn't help his rising spirits as he steered his horse toward the Stoltzfus residence.

No doubt, he'd see her family. Had she told them where they were going and why? Did they know of her wish to open a craft store, which she was closer to achieving? He knew that her sister Ellie was aware, for she'd told Isaac and Isaac had told him. But what of the others? Did they know? *They must.* Why else would she tell him that he could pick her up at her house? She wouldn't want them to think that they were seeing each other. His spirits dampened slightly as the truth—the reality—of their working relationship reminded him that while polite and even friendly toward him, Leah still didn't think much of him as a person.

The Stoltzfus residence loomed ahead, and he clenched his stomach. Henry slowed his horse, then steered him off the road onto Arlin's property. There were no buggies in the yard. Was that why Leah had allowed him to come? The notion hurt but he shouldn't have been surprised.

He tied up his horse and approached the house. He knocked on the back door and waited. If the Stoltzfus family were anything like his, they would spend a great deal of their time in the kitchen. There was no answer. He frowned. Had Leah gone out with her sisters? Had she forgotten that they were to meet this morning, that she'd agreed that he would accompany her to look for a store location?

He knocked again. When no one came after a few minutes, he headed toward the front door in case there was someone in that part of the house. He experienced a burning in his chest when it became clear that there was no one inside. He left the front of the house for his buggy. He had stepped up to climb inside when his gaze fell on the open doors of the barn. He knew a sudden lurch of fear. Leah clearly had been happy to learn everything he had to teach her. Surely, she hadn't forgotten their excursion.

He hurried toward the barn. Henry stepped inside and thought he heard a noise. A loud, strangled sound. Was an animal in trouble? A weight settled deeply inside his chest. Or was it Leah who was hurt?

He glanced in each stall as he moved farther into the barn. He heard a sob and he realized that it was coming from inside the stall where he'd installed the cabinet. He didn't see anyone at first, but then the heartbreaking sound of crying had him opening the stall door. And then he saw her. And she was clearly in a lot of pain. He rushed to hunker down at her side. "Leah, did you hurt yourself?"

At first, it seemed as if she hadn't heard him or realized that he was there. She was bent over, clutching her stomach, bawling.

"Leah." He touched her arm. She jerked back instinctively and lifted her head. She gazed at him for a long moment, then resumed crying.

He shifted to sit beside her. "Leah, tell me what's wrong. Maybe I can help you."

"I can't go with you," she finally whimpered. "Go home. I can't go right now."

"Talk to me. What is it?"

She leaned back, met his gaze. "I…"

"You can tell me. I won't tell anyone. You have my word." He prayed that she trusted him enough to confide in him.

"I was cleaning this morning," she began as she wiped her eyes. "Everyone had someplace to be, so I thought I'd help *Mam* and do some of the housework that needed to be done." She took a long shuddering breath before continuing. "I was cleaning my parents' room. I found a box under their bed." She met his gaze briefly, her eyes were filled with tears, before she looked away. "I was curious," she admitted, "so I took a look inside. I was happy to find school papers for me and my sisters." Her face crumpled at the word *sisters*, before she continued. "There were birth certificates inside for all my sisters, but not for me. But do you know what I found?"

Henry held her gaze, feeling tenderness toward Leah. He reached for her hand, and the fact that she didn't pull away told him how much something had hurt her.

"Adoption papers," she said, tears streaming down her cheeks. *"Mine."* She sniffed. "I'm not Arlin and Missy's daughter. I don't know who I am. I'm not a real part of the family."

"Leah," he whispered, aching for her, feeling suspiciously close to tears. "You are part of the family. I know that your parents love you."

"They're not my parents."

"They are your adoptive parents. They chose to keep you. That's something, isn't it?"

She shook her head as a spark of anger lit her glistening blue eyes. "*Nay*, 'tis not. They never told me. Maybe if I had known, this would be easier, but they kept it a secret from me. My sisters…" Her voice caught and he could tell that she couldn't go on.

"Love you," he said. His breath hitched. "*Your family* loves you."

"But that's just it—they aren't my family."

Henry opened his mouth to object, then decided to keep silent. Leah was feeling emotional and with good reason. All he could do was to be there for her. *So much for keeping my distance.* Studying her upturned, tear-streaked pretty face, he felt the strongest urge to take her into his arms. But he didn't have the right and he knew that she wouldn't welcome his embrace.

"Leah," he began carefully.

"I need to know who my parents are," she cried. "Why they abandoned me! How I cnded up here. I need to know, Henry. *I have to know!*"

He nodded. "I understand," he said. "I'd want the truth if it were me."

Her expression softened. "You would?"

"*Ja*, of course, I would, Leah, but—" He saw her look down at the hand that held hers and he quickly withdrew. "But you should talk with your parents—your adoptive parents," he corrected when her eyes hardened. "Question them. I know it hurts, but talk with them alone when you have the chance. I'm sure they'll be able to make you feel better about..."

"My adoption," she finished for him. He was glad to see that her features had relaxed again, as if her resolve to learn the truth from Arlin and Missy Stoltzfus had promised the hope of understanding.

"Shall we look at store locations? I don't want to push you," Henry said, "but today's search can help to keep you busy and perhaps make you feel better until they come home." He didn't make the mistake of saying *your family* or *adoptive parents*. Leah didn't need the reminder that might make her cry again. He rose to his feet and held out his hand to her. She gazed at it a moment before grasping his fingers. He quickly pulled her to stand beside him.

He smiled at her. "I have three places I'd like to show you." He didn't release her hand as he led her from the barn, then stopped to gaze at her. To his surprise she didn't pull away.

"You do?" She was close enough for him to see the dark blue flecks in her bright azure eyes. She wore a spring-green dress, which strengthened rather than distracted from the blue in her irises.

He was overly conscious of her nearness...her clean familiar scent of vanilla and honey soap laced pleasantly with her sweet-smelling shampoo. Her blond hair looked golden in the morning sunshine. Her lashes were dark for someone who was blonde. There were traces of tears on those eyelashes and drying remnants on her lovely smooth cheeks. He realized he was staring when he felt her shift uncomfortably. With an inward sigh, he let go of her fingers. "*Ja*. I can take you other places as well, but let's start with these three. *Oll recht?*" She swayed toward him and he gently grasped her shoulders. "Are you feeling well enough?"

"I'm fine," she assured him. "I'd like to go."

She didn't object when he helped her into the buggy. He shouldn't be happy at the sign that they were becoming friends, but he couldn't help himself.

Leah sat beside Henry as he drove his buggy to a second potential store location. The first stop seemed promising at first. It was on the main road through Happiness, down from Whittier's Store; only this building was farther out from her Amish community than she would have liked. Still, it remained a good possibility until they spoke with the English owner. Not only did the store need a lot of repair work, the owner, a Mr. Terence Brown, was asking too much for rent.

She climbed into the vehicle without a word. Henry got in beside her and flicked the leathers to head to the next location. "He wants too much money," he finally said after a few minutes of silence during the ride.

"Ja." She didn't look at him. The day had begun with anticipation and excitement which had suddenly turned dark when she'd discovered her adoption papers in her parents' room.

"We'll find you a better place."

She faced him, then bobbed her head.

"Don't think about it, Leah," he urged as if reading her mind about her adoption. "There will be time to talk with them later."

She released a sharp breath. "I know that, but—"

He reached across the wooden seat for her hand, interweaving his fingers through hers. His hand was warm and hard and strong. Her heart started to beat harder as she met his gaze. He was a handsome man. His blue eyes were filled with tenderness and compassion. His dark brown hair curled slightly beneath his black-banded straw hat. He wore a burgundy shirt with black tri-blend denim pants held up with black suspenders. The fact that she found him attractive frightened her. She trusted him to help her with the store, but she couldn't allow herself to think of anything more.

The fact that Isaac was friends again with Henry wasn't enough for her to entrust him with her heart.

"*Danki* for your concern," she murmured as she pulled her hand away. She immediately suffered from the loss of contact. She looked out the window, anywhere but at him. Leah could sense his regard, his disappointment, but she had to protect herself. Just because it looked as if she'd be an old maid without a family didn't meant she should grab the first man who paid her any attention.

"Leah."

She shot him a quick look. The sadness in his blue eyes was nearly her undoing. She didn't want to hurt him. She studied him for a long moment, then attempted to smile at him. When his expression brightened a little, she realized that her smile must have appeared genuine. Her caution nearly sifted away with the breeze.

"Danki," she heard him murmur moments later.

Studying the passing scenery out her side window, Leah closed her eyes. She hoped everything would be all right, but she didn't hold much hope that she'd ever feel the same way about her family and her home.

Ten minutes later, Henry steered the carriage into a paved parking lot near a small brick building which housed two different businesses. He got out, tied up his horse, then came around the vehicle to help.

Leah stared at the building and became aware of Henry's hand extended to assist her. She hesitated, unsure whether or not to touch those masculine fingers again. Then she recalled how nice it had felt to have him hold her hand earlier. She reached out to grab his hand and he helped her down. She felt an odd, disquieting disappointment when he released her quickly, as if he'd been burned by her touch. She shifted her gaze to the building and her surroundings. *Henry has been nothing but kind to me.* Why was she stressing over a simple offer of help? It wasn't as if he'd asked to be more than a teacher or a friend. But despite her resolve to be careful, she knew that a friendship was developing between them. While she cherished it, she also held herself back. Something had changed since this morning when he'd found her crying in the barn. She wasn't sure exactly what the shift between them meant yet.

Henry didn't say a word as together they approached the front door of the store that was empty. The entrance door opened as they drew near. A young woman in her early to midtwenties waited for them. "Sarah Richardson?" he asked.

"Yes, come in." The woman was a pretty *Englisher* wearing a long blue skirt with a white short-sleeved blouse. Leah saw the way Henry studied her and she felt jealous, which upset her since jealousy was a sin. And she didn't want to feel too much for Henry.

Sarah Richardson held the door open and Henry waited for Leah to precede him inside. Leah looked about the floor space, which appeared too small for what she had in mind.

"I apologize for the condition. My aunt used this space for a used bookstore." Sarah's brown eyes filled with sadness. "She passed away recently, and being her only relative, I'm in charge of her estate."

"I remember her store," Leah said. She softened her expression. "I'm sorry for your loss." She turned back to examine the interior critically. She'd never been inside. "How much space is there in the back?"

Sarah seemed surprised that Leah had asked and not Henry. Leah looked at him, saw the amused twinkle in his blue eyes and the slight upward tilt of his beautiful male mouth.

"I'm the one looking to rent store space," Leah explained. "For a craft shop."

Sarah pulled her gaze from Henry to stare at her. "There's a fair amount of space in the back. Would you like to see?"

Leah nodded. She tried to picture crafts and supplies on shelves and on the floor in this building, but something was lacking. The space just wasn't right for her. Still, she wanted to see the back. Perhaps if the back room was large enough, she could have a wall moved back to create a larger merchandise area.

She trailed behind Sarah, aware of Henry following closely. Leah felt a tingling at the back of her neck, overly aware of his penetrating gaze on her. She halted to glance back, then was disappointed when she realized that he'd been studying Sarah and not her.

Leah perused the rear work area and was pleased to see that it was much larger than she'd expected. This store could work if Sarah was willing to renovate the store space. "This is a lot of space back here. Would you be willing to move this wall back a little to allow for a larger front merchandise area?"

Sarah's mouth dropped open. "You want to move a wall? Are you kidding me?"

Stiffening, Leah said, "No, I'm serious. You have more space back here than in the storefront. I need more space for merchandise." She paused. "I think you'll find others will feel the same way."

The woman, to her credit, appeared to give the matter some thought. "I'll have to look into this further and get back with you."

"How much are you asking for rent?"

Sarah named a figure that could be doable, but there was a lot to consider before Leah agreed.

"Leah," Henry said softly. "We should go. 'Tis getting late and we have one other place to see today."

Meeting his gaze, she nodded before turning toward Sarah. "Thank you for your time."

"Is there a way for me to reach you? In the event, that I'm willing to move the wall?"

Henry handed the woman a paper with a name and phone number. "That's the number for Whittier's Store. Leave a message with Bob that you need to speak with Leah and she'll call you back."

The *Englisher* accepted the phone number, then walked with them to the front entrance. "Thank you for coming," she said pleasantly.

Henry spoke up before Leah had a chance. "We appreciate your time."

Thoughtful, Leah walked to the buggy in silence. She quickly climbed in before Henry could extend an assisting hand. She knew she shouldn't be feeling annoyed or ungrateful that he'd spoken up on her behalf, but her world was turned upside down and she needed to take charge, at least, in the one aspect of her life that she could—her craft store.

She waited while Henry untied his horse, then climbed in next to her. He didn't say a word as he grabbed the leathers and steered the horse back onto the main road. They had one more stop to make, but Leah was no longer in the mood. She felt testy and could no longer put her upcoming talk with her adoptive parents from her mind.

"Henry, please take me home."

She felt him stiffen before he glanced in her direction.

Her gaze pleaded for understanding. "Please, Henry."

He regarded her a long moment, his expression unreadable, before he gave a nod. Within minutes, Leah saw the house ahead and the buggy in their driveway. Her adoptive parents were home, and most likely her sisters were there, too. "Stop!" she cried urgently.

He drew sharply on the reins. "What's wrong?" He gazed at her, clearly wondering about her outburst.

"Would you let me out here? My parents are home."

He appeared hurt for a brief moment, a look that was gone so quickly she couldn't be sure she hadn't imagined it.

"I'll be in touch." Her lip quivered and she started to shake. "Wish me luck," she whispered.

His expression softened. "You don't need luck, Leah," he said. "Just be honest and ask what you need to know."

"I—" She paused, warmed by his understanding. "May I come by next Tuesday?" She bit her lip. "The store?"

He shook his head regretfully. "I don't know if I'll be

at the store. I've got other work to do and *Mam* wants to work."

She nodded. Was he telling the truth about having other plans? Or did he just not want to see her again?

With a murmur of thanks, Leah climbed out of the carriage and walked toward the house. Alone on the road, she looked back in time to see Henry turn the buggy around and head home. *I've upset him*, she realized. She might have even made him angry. But she was so hurt and confused by the discovery of her adoption papers that she couldn't think straight. Yet, right after that thought, she couldn't stop the niggle of concern that Henry might be upset and not want to see her again.

She reached the barnyard within minutes, just as Charlie came bounding out the back door. Her youngest sister spied her and ran in her direction. "Leah! Everyone's been wondering where you went."

Leah managed a smile. "I had an errand to run."

"Where?"

"Nowhere important," she answered vaguely. "*Mam* and *Dat* inside?"

Charlie nodded. "*Mam's* making a late lunch. We all just got back. Ellie should be home soon, too."

She gazed at the house. "And *Dat*?"

Her sister beamed at her. "He's in the barn with the puppy."

Leah felt herself soften. "Nell brought him," she murmured. "I thought he was too young."

"*Nay*, James thought he'd be fine. And Nell didn't bring him. *Dat* picked him up from their *haus*."

"Is he alone?"

Charlie looked at her strangely. "*Ja*. Why?"

"Nothing. I thought he might want some time alone with the new dog before I barge in to take a look."

"*Dat* won't mind if you visit Jeremiah."

"Jeremiah?" Leah arched an eyebrow.

"*Ja.* I think 'tis a *gut* name, don't you?"

"Let me guess. You came up with it."

Her sister shrugged. "Maybe, but *Dat* seemed to think it a fine name for our new member of our animal family."

The mention of family darkened the light in Leah's heart. "I think I'll go inside to see if *Mam* needs help with lunch." Then, without waiting for Charlie's reaction, Leah escaped into the house, asked Missy if she needed assistance, then when Missy said no, she hurried to her room to catch her breath and compose herself. Until she had a private moment to discuss what she'd found, she would have to act naturally around her adoptive family. No matter how hard it would be to do so.

Leah stood at her window, staring outside, wondering how she would broach the subject of her adoption. She had a lump in her throat, and her eyes were moist from her recent bout with tears. But she was no longer crying and she wouldn't again. This evening she would have to find the time to talk with her parents alone.

"Leah." Charlie stepped inside the room. "Lunch is ready."

She turned from the view and managed to smile. "I'll be right down."

Her sister hesitated. "You're upset about something."

Leah shook her head. "I'm fine."

"You seem pensive. As if something is weighing on your mind."

"You don't have to worry about me, Charlie." Her sister's concern made Leah's smile more genuine.

Charlie studied her a moment, then nodded. "Come downstairs. Before Ellie plows through the meal to get to the dessert." She started toward the door. "I made a chocolate cake," she said over her shoulder.

"We can't have her eating all the cake now, can we?" Leah said, unable to keep from being amused at the younger woman.

They ate sandwiches and salads for the midday meal. When they were done, Charlie proudly brought out the cake she'd baked. The family ate amid conversation, laughter and grins. Leah was quieter than usual but no one seemed to notice. She knew that at some point today she'd have to confront her adoptive parents and get answers to the serious questions and concerns that she had.

Ellie had gone back to work. She had another cleaning job to do. Although it wasn't a particularly large one, she'd asked Leah if she wanted to help since she knew that Leah was working to save money.

"Can't this afternoon," Leah had said with a smile before Ellie left. "I have a few things I need to do today."

Charlie had been asked by their cousin Jedidiah if she'd help out his wife, Sarah, today. She'd met him as on her way home from the Abram Peachy residence earlier. Sarah was pregnant with her third child, and she needed Charlie's help with the other children since she wasn't feeling well lately.

With both sisters gone, Leah was finally able to talk with her parents alone.

"*Mam. Dat.* May I speak with you?" she asked grimly.

Arlin, who'd been heading for the back door, returned to sit at the head of thc kitchen table. "What's on your mind, *dochter*?"

His use of *daughter* had her closing her eyes in pain.

"Leah," Missy said as she sat near her husband and across from Leah. "What's happened?" She gazed at her with concern.

Her heart started to pound as she eyed the two people who, she'd thought, were her parents. "I was cleaning your room this morning, and I found something under your bed."

After he'd dropped off Leah, Henry headed toward home. It hurt him that she didn't want her family to see them together. It was as if she were ashamed of him. Did she regard him so poorly that she was afraid to let her family know of their working relationship? Or was it because her parents didn't know that she wanted to own a craft business?

"'Tis a *gut* thing she doesn't know how I'm starting to feel toward her," he murmured. The store loomed up ahead. His mother had brought his father with her to work this morning. Before he'd left earlier, he'd helped his *dat* get settled in a chair by the front counter. He'd also made sure that there was a more comfortable chair in the back room for when his father became too tired to deal with customers. Henry had planned to drive past and up toward the barn where he usually worked on his cabinets, but concern for his parents had him parking close to the store. He tied up his horse before he went inside. He saw his mother behind the counter. Next to her, where others could see him, sat his father. He appeared happy to be in the store, his eyes clear and his expression bright. Charlotte Peachy was paying for her purchases and she and his parents were having a conversation. Charlotte had been a kind girl when younger, and she hadn't changed. After his parents acknowledged him as he approached, the deacon's wife turned to grin at him.

"Henry!" she greeted with a warm smile. "I was catching up with your *eldre*. I'm glad your *dat* is doing well." Her eyes met his father's for a heartbeat before she shifted her gaze back to him. "I was just telling them how glad I am that they'll be returning to our church community. We've missed all of you. I know that Isaac is happy to have you back. And Ellen can't say enough *gut* things about you." She picked up her bag of groceries, then turned to face him. "I heard, from Arlin, that you made him a cabinet. I was wondering if you'd be willing to stop by. I have a small job I hope you'll be interested in."

His parents looked at him approvingly. Henry nodded. "When would you like me to come?" he asked, his gaze meeting those of his parents to ensure that he hadn't misread their expressions. His *mam* was smiling at him, while his *dat* beamed, clearly pleased.

"Next Tuesday? Around two?"

"I'll be there," Henry told her. He experienced a burst of excitement as he watched Charlotte leave. He faced his parents. "Do you need anything from the *haus*? I thought I'd work a bit in the barn."

"Go ahead," his father said. "We have everything we could possibly need right here in the store."

Henry went into the barn, stared at a project he'd been working on as a surprise for Isaac and Ellen, and tried to forget the pain he'd felt in knowing that Leah didn't want her family to know that they'd spent time together.

Chapter Seven

Leah sat across from her parents, her eyes dry, as she'd explained about the papers she'd found that morning. "You adopted me, and you never told me." She saw Missy and Arlin exchange horrified, guilty looks. "I want to know who my parents are. I want to know how I came to be in your care. I want to know why you hid the fact that I'm not your *dochter*!"

"Leah, you *are* our daughter," her mother said. "We love you."

"Leah—" Her father stood, paced about the room. "You know we love you. We didn't tell you because you are *our* daughter. You must know we think of you as our own."

"Do you know how it felt to learn about it in that way? Maybe I shouldn't have looked inside the box, but I didn't think there was really anything to hide. I saw all the papers we'd done in school. Then I found your daughters' birth certificates and wondered if mine was in the pile. So I dug a little deeper and that's when I found the adoption papers." She blinked against tears.

"Who am I?" she whispered. "What happened to my parents? They didn't want me?"

"Nay!" Missy cried as she shoved back her chair. "It wasn't that."

"Missy," her husband warned.

Leah blinked back tears. "Why won't you tell me?"

Arlin gazed at her kindly. "We can't," he said softly.

"Can't?" she cried. "Or won't?"

"Both." He grabbed his hat from a wall peg and opened the back door.

"You're just going to leave without giving me any answers?"

"I can't tell you what you want to know." Suddenly stoic, he shoved his hat on his head and exited the house, leaving Leah alone with Missy.

Despite her determination not to cry, Leah felt tears running down her cheeks as she turned toward her adoptive mother. *"Mam?"*

But Missy looked away. "I'm sorry. We can't," she breathed as she stared at her. "I have things to do. Leah, we love you. I hope you believe us and accept that we want only what's best for you." Then she left the room, and Leah could hear the sound of her footsteps on the wooden stairs as she went up to the second floor. No doubt to hide the box that Leah had found, so she'd have no other opportunity to look at it again and maybe discover some pertinent information she might have missed.

Left alone in the kitchen without answers, she was overwhelmed with grief. She felt betrayed. Her parents were not hers at all, but some strangers who had taken her in to live with them. She recalled how they'd pressed their daughter Nell to marry, how pleased they'd been when Meg had fallen in love and wedded Peter Zook. They had even talked about Ellie and Charlie marrying someday, but never her. Which was why she'd decided that they didn't care whether or not she married. As if she wasn't good enough to be a man's wife and mother to his children.

Leah had to get out of the house. She needed to talk with Henry. He was the only one besides Missy and Arlin who knew what she'd found. She ran outside, relieved to see that the pony cart was in the yard. Within minutes, she was headed to Yoder's General Store. Henry would understand. He would figure out a way to help her. She bit her lip. *I hope.*

When she pulled her vehicle into the store parking lot, she noticed that there were no other buggies around. She tied up her horse, got out and headed inside. Henry had said that his mother was working in the store today. Perhaps Henry decided to help her after he'd dropped her off.

She felt a wave of remorse. When she'd seen that her parents were home, she'd ordered Henry to stop and let her out. Had he understood why? Because she was nervous about confronting her adoptive parents? A knot formed in her belly. Did he think otherwise? She hoped he didn't believe that she was ashamed to be seen with him. But with her other worries, it didn't seem like the best time to tell her adoptive parents why she'd been out riding with him.

Concern made her feel jittery as she fingered the doorknob to the front entrance. She heard the bell on the door jingle as she pulled it open and stepped inside. Henry's mother had allowed the goat bell to remain on the door, believing her son's idea to be a good one.

There was no one near the counter. Leah saw a chair beside it and wondered if that wasn't where Henry's father had sat while his wife, Margaret, had waited on customers. She frowned. Where was she? She hoped that Harry hadn't had a relapse.

"Hallo?" she called out as she moved closer to the counter. "Is anyone here?"

A figure came out from the back room. "Leah!" It was Henry's mother. "I'm sorry, I didn't hear the bell."

Leah glanced at the chair. "Is Harry *oll recht*?"

"He's fine." Margaret smiled, which reassured her. "I sent him up to the *haus* to rest." She tilted her head as she studied her, perhaps noting Leah's tension. "What can I get you?"

Leah thought quickly for something that was needed at home until she began to wonder if she could remain with the Stoltzfuses now that she knew the truth. Her mind went blank. "I'm not here to shop," she admitted honestly. "I was looking for Henry. Is he around?"

"He's up at the *haus* with Harry."

"I see." She wouldn't disturb him then. Besides, it wasn't as if she had the right to seek his help. They were just learning to become friends. "I don't want to bother him. I should go."

"Wait!" Margaret called as Leah started toward the door. "Why don't you go up and see him? I'm sure he'll be pleased to see you."

Leah froze. What was she doing? Coming to talk with Henry? She suddenly regretted seeking him out, especially after the way she'd treated him initially. "'Tis nothing important. I'll talk with him another time."

"I'm about to close the store. Are you sure you won't come up to the *haus* with me?"

"Nay." She managed to smile. She turned to leave, then paused. "I'm glad Harry is doing well." She hurried from the store, climbed into the cart and left. She'd driven a mile or more down the road when she heard the sound of another horse-drawn vehicle behind her.

"Leah!" It was Henry.

She slowed her horse and pulled it safely onto the shoulder of the road. Henry waved as he steered his buggy past her before he parked his wagon in front of her cart.

"Henry." She met his gaze and hid the fact that she was glad to see him, even though the knowledge that his mother must have told him embarrassed her.

He climbed out and approached. "You should have come up to the *haus*."

She felt a lump rise in her throat. "You were with your *vadder*. I didn't want to bother you."

He studied her a moment. "You're no bother," he said. He frowned. "Did you talk to them?"

She was unable to meet his gaze.

"Leah." The fact that he could tell she was upset should have bothered her, but it didn't.

"*Ja*, I spoke with my parents," she confessed, her eyes locking with his. The memory of their discussion, or lack thereof, made her choke up. "It didn't go well," she whispered. The understanding in his expression nearly made her cry.

He held out his hand. "Let's go for a walk," he urged.

She looked at their vehicles. "We can't leave our buggies here."

"We'll pull in behind Millie Mast's bakery. She won't mind. We can take a short walk from there." The look in his sky blue eyes was warm and encouraging. "The horses will be fine. There's a hitching post in the back."

Leah stared back at him a long moment, then gave a nod. They climbed into their vehicles, and she followed Henry down the road until they reached the bakery. She was familiar with the place. Her brother-in-law James had lived in an apartment above the bakery when he'd been operating his veterinary clinic—before he'd joined the Amish church and married Nell. Now she believed Andrew Brighton, James's friend from veterinary school, lived there. He'd taken over the clinic while James kept his work helping animals within their community. He gave medical care to English farmers' animals as well, when they needed him and if they couldn't get a hold of Drew.

Leah pulled her cart into the lot behind Henry's wagon, then tied up her horse next to his. "Where would you like to walk?" She suddenly felt shy. Could she do this? Tell him about her conversation with her parents? And, most important, could she trust him? For some strange reason, she knew she could.

"We don't have to walk," he said. "Look. There's a bench over there."

She glanced over. Sure enough there was a wooden bench under a shade tree. It must be new since she didn't remember seeing it the last time she'd bought something from Millie's bakery.

The bench looked inviting, but still she hesitated.

"Leah?" He held out his hand, and, heart racing hard, she paused for a just a second to stare at it before she took it. The warmth of his fingers clasping hers soothed her.

She sat on the bench and Henry settled next to her. Without releasing her hand.

She was quiet a long moment, unable to speak as she fought tears. *Nay!* she thought. She wouldn't cry. She couldn't cry and explain what happened. Henry squeezed her hand and she looked at him. His expression encouraged, his smile was gentle. He was so handsome he stole her breath, but the thought was fleeting, for, as hard as this would be, she had to tell someone. She wanted to tell him.

Leah closed her eyes briefly. "They won't say," she blurted out.

Henry felt his heart break for Leah as he glimpsed the tears in her eyes. "Won't say what?" he asked.

She pulled away and stood. "They won't tell me anything about my birth parents. They said they love me and basically that I should accept that." She sniffed and tears escaped to trail down her smooth cheeks as she faced him. "*Dat* walked out of the *haus* in the middle of the conversation." She met his gaze, her blue eyes glistening. "*Mam* said she had work to do and left."

He wanted to rise and take her into his arms to comfort her but didn't. "I'm sorry," he whispered.

She tried to smile but failed. "I don't know what to do. I want to know. I *have* to know."

Henry nodded. "Give them time. What if legally they can't tell you. They might have to get permission first."

"But it's my life. I'm an adult and old enough to know." She returned to her seat beside him.

He reached for her hand and was glad when she didn't pull away but turned her palm up and laced her fingers with his. "Do you think 'tis because they want to protect you? I believe that they love you as their own.

I've seen the love in Arlin's eyes—a *vadder's* love for his *dochter*."

She withdrew her hand and rose. He fought the feeling of hurt at the distance. "This is hard for me. I know in my heart that they love me. They wouldn't have cared for me all these years, but..." She paced a few steps and paused, then returned and sat down again. "It still hurts," she whispered.

"I know." He softened his expression as he felt the strongest urge offer comfort her, to confront Arlin and Missy and demand answers. But he couldn't, of course. The only thing he could do was be there for her, to listen and be a sympathetic ear. "I'd wait a day or two, then ask again. Make them see how important this is to you." When she shot him a hopeful look, he added, "I think it would be worth taking the chance, don't you?"

Looking relieved, she bobbed her head.

He smiled at her. "Would you like a soda or—" he grinned "—a cup of tea?"

To his amazement, she laughed. "Hot tea?"

He stood, reached to help her rise. It seemed natural when she followed his lead. "Is there any other kind of tea?" He glanced toward the bakery. "And I'd like to buy you a cupcake."

"I wouldn't mind a chocolate one."

They headed toward the bakery, where he ordered two chocolate cupcakes and hot tea. When they got their order, they returned to the bench to enjoy the snack. Henry took a bite of the delicious chocolate cake and made a sound of pleasure. "These are *gut*," he said. "So what are you going to do?"

He watched her swallow a mouthful of cake before

she answered. "I'm going to take your advice. Wait for a while, then ask again."

"Gut." He eyed her with approval as he popped the last of his cupcake into his mouth and swallowed. "Want to keep looking for a place of your store?"

Leah was thoughtful for several moments. "I'd like that."

Henry beamed at her, overjoyed at the prospect of more time with her. "When?"

"Monday?"

He agreed. "I'll wait for you at the store."

"Henry," she began, looking apologetic. "I'm sorry." She bit her lip. "For not asking you to come in with me when we reached the *haus*. I realized afterward what you must have thought after I asked you to stop and let me out. But it wasn't because I was uncomfortable to be seen with you. It was because…" She inhaled sharply before continuing. "When I saw my parents, all I could think of was that I wasn't their daughter and it hurt."

"I understand," he said. And he truly did. She'd been overwhelmed after learning of her adoption and worried about confronting her parents. The fact that she had come to the store later to talk with him, that she had confided in him with her secret fears made him feel a whole lot better. And it meant a lot to him that she'd decided to take his advice and wait before talking about her adoption with Missy and Arlin.

With both cupcakes consumed, they went their separate ways after setting up a time to go store hunting again on Monday morning, which would work out fine since he promised to go to the Peachy residence about a job on Tuesday. Henry smiled as he watched Leah's departure. All he'd ever wanted was for her to accept him as someone other than the one who had betrayed her cousin. The fact that she'd turned to him today was an indication that she had begun to regard him as a friend. *Thanks be to God.*

Leah decided that she couldn't go store hunting with Henry on Monday. The more she thought about what she'd told him, the more she felt embarrassed, and she felt it would be wise to put some distance between them. Not that she was afraid he'd break her confidence. He'd promised to keep her secret, and she believed him. But there was no reason to look for a location when the last thing on her mind at this point was her opening a craft shop. So Leah debated about writing him a note and asking her sister Ellie to deliver it for her, but she realized that she should tell him in person this weekend when she saw him. She tried not to feel bad that she'd let Henry down by canceling their plans. It was only hours since she'd approached her adoptive parents with the knowledge of her adoption. She figured next week would be enough time passed for her to ask them again about her birth parents. Unfortunately, Missy and Arlin Stoltzfus clearly didn't want to talk. Since Leah had brought up the subject, they continued to keep their distance. With a sound of frustration, Leah went to check on their new dog in his barn stall. She wanted to visit with the little one, hoping she'd feel better rather than out of sorts.

It was already getting dark. With a flashlight in hand, she pulled open the one side of barn doors, then entered and headed toward Jeremiah's area. She peeked in, expecting to see the puppy curled up and sleeping. She froze and gasped. What she hadn't expected was to find that he wasn't alone. A young girl lay next to the little dog. An *Englisher* by the looks of her. She appeared to be in her teens. She lay, curled on her side with Jeremiah snuggled against her. As if sensing a presence, the girl's eyes suddenly opened. When she saw Leah, she quickly scrambled to her feet, her movements waking up Jeremiah.

"I'm sorry," the teenager said. "I know I shouldn't be here." Eyeing Leah warily, she edged toward the stall door. "I was tired and fell asleep. I'll just be on my way."

Her shock dissipated. "Who are you?" Leah asked.

"It doesn't matter," she murmured. "Can't I just go? *Please.* I promise I won't bother you again."

It was then that Leah realized from her rumpled clothes, dirty face and frightened expression that the girl was a runaway. "I can help you."

The young *Englisher* shook her head no. "I'm fine. I shouldn't have come here." She paused. "But I was so tired and thought only to lie down for a minute."

"Where do you live?" Leah asked. The stark terror that entered the girl's eyes and the way she hugged herself with her arms told her that the girl had escaped from a bad home situation. "You're safe here."

The girl stared as if debating whether or not to believe her. "Jess," she murmured. "My name's Jessica."

"Are you hungry, Jess?" Leah asked gently.

"I have to leave—"

Leah stepped back to allow the girl to exit the stall. "Go ahead. But if you're hungry, I can grab you some snacks from the house."

Jess stepped out of the stall, making sure she closed the door so that Jeremiah wouldn't escape. "Everyone is inside. If I hurry, I can get you food to take with you before you go." She hesitated. "Or you could stay the night and leave first thing. I won't tell anyone."

The girl frowned. "I don't know…"

"It's up to you. I won't force you." She sensed the moment when Jess started to lower her guard and relax. "Do you want something to eat?"

"I can't stay."

"You don't have to," Leah assured her. "You can leave while I go inside if you want, but I hope you'll wait for me." She smiled. "I'll be quick."

Jess nodded. "Okay."

Leah ran out of the barn and hurried into the house. Fortunately, there was no one in kitchen. She grabbed cookies and an apple, then added a few slices of bread and cheese. It wasn't much, but she'd bet that it was more than Jess had eaten in a while. She found a plastic bag and stuffed the food inside, then reached for a can of soda, the kind her sister Charlie preferred. On impulse, she stuck a flashlight in the bag before she rushed back to the barn. She must have made noise as she approached, because the girl gasped, spun and looked terrified until she recognized Leah.

"I put a few things in here for you," she said as she offered Jess the bag. "There's a flashlight in there, too."

She saw Jess blink back tears. "Thank you."

"Sleep. Just leave at dawn. If you come back to sleep again, make sure you come after dark and enter through the back door." Leah regarded her with compassion. "That's how you got in, isn't it?" The girl nodded. "I'm Leah Stoltzfus."

Jess gazed at her a long moment. "Thank you, Leah." A horse snorted in a nearby stall, startling her.

"Take care of yourself, Jess," Leah said softly. "If you ever need help, come find me."

"I can't stay. I need to go," Jess cried. With the bag clutched tightly against her, she fled past Leah as if she were being chased by wolves.

Leah fought the urge to run after her or to watch which direction she'd taken. The girl needed sleep and she was in serious trouble. While she would have liked nothing more than to run after her, Leah hung back. She entered Jeremiah's stall and hunkered down in the straw beside him. The puppy, who'd been whimpering since he'd woken up, quieted when she sat and pulled him onto her lap. As she ran her fingers through the dog's fur, she thought of Jess and wondered if the girl had slept here previously without discovery. She had believed that Charlie had been the one who'd messed up the straw after she'd put in a fresh bed before Jeremiah's arrival.

What if it had been Jess? What if she'd slept more than one night here? And if she had, what made her risk discovery by sleeping here during the day?

She spent several minutes running her fingers through Jeremiah's fur. After he fell asleep, she carefully moved their puppy onto his new bed. As she left the barn, she saw and she heard a buggy approaching along the dirt lane from the main road. Who could it be at this hour?

Was it the church bench wagon? Jess had left just in time. As thoughts of the girl entered her mind, Leah hesitated. Considering what the girl had suffered, she realized that she shouldn't be upset that she was adopted. Her adoptive parents had given her a good, loving home.

They didn't deserve for her to hurt them by continuing to bring up her past.

Leah sighed. She only wanted to have a sense of who she was. And what had happened to her birth parents. What was wrong with that?

Henry steered his horse down the lane leading to the Arlin Stoltzfus residence. He probably shouldn't have come. It was late. But he wanted to see Leah. He was worried about her and needed to make sure she was all right.

What if she just doesn't want to see me?

He felt a burning in his stomach. He'd thought they'd become friends. What if she had changed her mind about him? What if she no longer trusted him? If she regretted confiding in him? A shaft of pain enveloped him at the thought.

He saw the beam of a flashlight as someone exited the barn as he drove past the house. The person moved and he recognized Leah in the flash of light. She stared at his buggy, but he was unable to gauge her reaction to his visit. He parked and got out of the vehicle. "Leah."

She closed her eyes and released a sharp breath. "Henry, it's late," she said quietly. "I didn't expect to see you."

He approached, stopping within a few feet of her, and studied her with concern. The golden glow of the light softened her face, making her appear extremely vulnerable. "I know. I'm sorry if I'm intruding but I wanted to make sure you were *oll recht*."

"That's kind of you."

Henry continued to enjoy the sight of her. She didn't seem overly upset that he'd come…unless she was good at hiding her feelings. "What is going on?" he asked worriedly.

She shot a look toward the house. "Nothing." She bit her lip.

"Have they said anything?"

"*Nay*, I thought I'd try talking with them again next week." Her blue eyes filled with hurt. "They are avoiding me." Her voice lowered. "Except for supper, after which, they left the room so they didn't have to be alone with me."

Henry regarded her with compassion. "They are afraid to talk about it."

"Ja." She stepped away from the barn.

He noticed that her hair and skin appeared more golden in the flashlight's beam. "Is there anything I can do?"

She shook her head and gazed at him through worried eyes. "I was going to send you a note. About next week. Then I thought I'd tell you in person. I think it's wise if I put any store plans on hold."

He stared at her, noting her discomfort. "You want to forget about our lessons and looking for a location." He was more than a little disappointed. He'd been looking forward to spending more time with her. "I see," he murmured. "I hope you'll ask for my help when you're ready to begin again."

When she didn't immediately agree, Henry felt his spirits sink to an all-time low.

"I should go," he said. It was clear that Leah was tired of his company, had changed her mind about their working arrangement. She didn't say a word as he climbed into his buggy.

He was stunned when she approached his buggy window. "Henry," she began, "will I see you on Sunday?"

His heart, which had picked up its pace when she approached, slowed. "*Ja*, my *dat* is well enough for church service." He picked up the reins and clicked his tongue to get his vehicle moving. "Take care, Leah. I'll see you then." He steered the horse toward the road and had traveled several yards when he heard Leah calling him. He quickly drew up on the leathers, then stuck his head out the window to see her running toward him. "Leah?" he asked with concern.

"I wanted to thank you for all you've done for me," she said softly.

"I haven't done anything—"

"Henry," she interrupted. "You've done more than you know, and I appreciate it."

Why was she thanking him now? He hadn't done anything. Was it because she no longer needed—or wanted—his help? Was this, in essence, a goodbye? "I didn't do anything."

"You're wrong! You sheltered me during the storm… and you taught me a lot about bookkeeping."

"Not that much, Leah," he said. "There's much more for you to learn."

"I know, but I just can't right now."

He understood the silent message. She didn't want to work with him. "I'll see you at church service." Then he flicked the leathers and headed for home.

He'd steered his horse about a mile down the road when a car came up from behind him and slowed. Henry glanced over and suffered a moment of dread.

"Henry Yoder," a male voice mocked with a cruel expression. "You and me need to talk." Then the *En-*

glisher pulled his car over to block off his escape, and Henry had no choice but to park on the side of the road and face his former friend. The same man who threatened to hurt his family and Isaac if Henry told the truth to the authorities about who had vandalized Whittier's Store that night years before.

"Brad Smith," he greeted, hiding his misgivings. "What are you doing out of jail?"

The man's expression hardened. "Aren't you happy to see an old friend?"

Chapter Eight

Midday Saturday was a flurry of activity in the Arlin Stoltzfus household. Leah, her mother and sisters had cleaned the day before. This morning, they put a roast in to cook and made a few dishes to add to the mid-day meal that everyone would partake of after church service the next day. Her uncle and male cousins had arrived a short time ago with the bench wagon. The men were clearing the furniture from the great room in readiness for the church benches.

Leah checked on the roast beef in the oven before she poured four glasses of iced tea for the men and then went into the great room to see how they were making out. Many of the benches were already set in place. She smiled at her uncle as she extended the tray of glasses toward him. Samuel Lapp accepted one with a nod of thanks. "Looks *gut*."

Her father approached from the other side of the room. *"Wunderbor, dochter. Danki."*

She grinned, happy with his pleasure. "Where's Isaac?"

"He's outside, waiting for Henry," her cousin Daniel

said as he accepted a glass of tea. “Not sure what’s taking him so long.”

“Henry’s coming?” Hearing mention of Henry made her heart skip a beat. He hadn’t mentioned that he’d be coming today.

“*Ja*, he’ll be helping with the benches.”

Leah nodded. She wanted to talk with her cousin before Henry arrived. Leah smiled at Daniel before she went outside. “Isaac.”

Her cousin Isaac turned from the bench wagon. He had slid out two benches and was reaching inside for another. “Leah!” His eyes lit up as he studied her.

“I thought you might be thirsty.”

He smiled. “I am. *Danki*.”

She nodded, then watched as he took a large swallow of the cold tea. “You told Henry about my hope of opening a craft shop,” she accused mildly.

He froze in the act of taking another drink to eye her over the glass. “*Ja*, I thought he could help you.”

She inclined her head. “I accepted his offer of help, and I already had my first lesson.”

Her cousin’s brow cleared. “*Gut*. That’s *gut*.”

“Ellie shouldn’t have told you.”

He shot her a surprised look. “She didn’t run to tell me, Leah. It simply came up in conversation. No one else knows.”

Leah scowled. “Except Henry.”

“But you accepted his help.”

“*Ja*, I did but—” How could she tell him that she’d put her plans on hold without telling him why? That she was upset to learn she’d been adopted?

“Leah, if the end result worked out, why are you

worrying? What do you have against Henry Yoder?" he asked, clearly puzzled.

She said the first thing that came to mind. "He hurt you." She set the tea tray on the empty side of the wagon. "You suffered because of him."

"Henry apologized and we're fine. If I can forgive him, why can't you?"

"I have forgiven him," she mumbled, sincere. Spending time in his company had made her see him for the kind man he actually was. She had skipped out on their recent plans to find her a place for her store, and she felt terrible about it. And she'd been thinking way too much about him… She wanted to know what had happened that night. The Henry she'd come to know didn't seem like the kind of man who destroyed other people's property, especially a friend's.

Isaac leaned against the back of the wagon. "There is more to what happened at the store that night."

"What happened?" Leah asked, intrigued.

Isaac shook his head. "Not my story to tell." He took another gulp of tea, then lowered his glass.

A buggy drove into the yard, drawing her attention. She felt nervous suddenly. It was Henry, come to help set up the church benches.

"I wouldn't suggest asking him about it, Leah," her cousin warned softly as Henry got out of his vehicle and waved. "It's still a painful subject for him. He doesn't need you digging into his thoughts. If he wants to tell you what happened that night at Whittier's Store, he will, but it will come from him when the time is right and not before." He steadily held her gaze.

She released a breath. "I understand," she said softly.

Her cousin grinned at her before they both turned to greet Henry.

"Isaac," Henry said as he approached. "Leah." His voice had turned noticeably cool.

Leah frowned. Their discussion last night had clearly upset him. Was he upset because she'd put off her lessons? Last night he hadn't seemed to be. He'd said he understood.

He stared at her without a word. Leah shifted uncomfortably, wishing she could turn back the clock and change how things stood between them.

Obviously uncomfortable with the sudden tension between her and his friend, Isaac cleared his throat. "Come on, Henry. These benches won't get into the house by themselves."

Leah started toward the house, then stopped to watch as each man lifted a wooden church bench from the wagon. Her attention was drawn immediately to Henry. She couldn't help but notice the play of arm muscles below his shirt's short sleeves. When he turned to set the bench down, he looked surprised to see her, as if wondering why she hadn't gone into the house. Blushing, she quickly looked away and hurried inside.

She was in the great room when she felt Henry's presence as soon as he entered. He carried the bench under one arm. There was a light sheen of perspiration on his forehead, and the dampness caused a lock of dark hair to curl. He barely looked at her as he set the bench next to another to finish one church row. As he turned to leave, he locked gazes with her, and she felt the intensity of his look ripple along her spine.

"Is there something you need?" she asked.

A shutter came over his expression. *"Nay."* He sighed.

"Henry, what's wrong? I can tell something is bothering you."

He shrugged. "Nothing for you—or anyone—to worry about." Then he left to get another church bench.

She was ready with glasses of iced tea and lunch when the men were done setting up the benches and had gone outside to enjoy the balmy day. She fought to hold her hand steady as she handed Henry one of the glasses.

Henry held her gaze as he took it from her. "*Danki*, Leah."

She nodded, then gave him his sandwich and quickly turned away to give Isaac and the others theirs. She could sense Henry's eyes on her as she returned to the house.

Her mother was in the kitchen as she entered. "Everyone get what they need?"

"*Ja*, although I think *Dat* will want some cookies," Leah replied with a smile.

"Here," *Mam* said as she held out a plate of cookies. "Take these out to them. I'm sure your *vadder* isn't the only who'll be interested in something sweet."

Leah felt heat surge in her belly as she carried the plate outside and heard the murmurs of pleasure when the men saw the cookies. "Everyone have enough iced tea?" she asked as she set it down on the tail end of the bench wagon. Surrounded by men, she was only conscious of Henry's nearness. "Another sandwich?" She glanced at each of them, surprised to find Henry's lips curved in a funny little smile.

"These are fine," he assured her, and the others immediately agreed.

Feeling her face warm, she murmured something appropriate and started to leave.

"Leah." Henry had followed her.

"Something I can help you with?" She glanced back quickly, glad to see that none of the others had noticed, except for Isaac, who wore a grin. She returned her attention to Henry.

"I just wanted to thank you again for lunch," he said, his expression unreadable.

"You're *willkoom*." She became flustered when he stared at her without moving. "Henry?" She wanted to repair their budding friendship. She hated the sudden tension that had cropped up since he'd arrived this morning.

"I'll see you at church service tomorrow."

She managed a polite smile. Her mouth felt stiff and unnatural. "I'll see you then." She turned.

"Leah."

Heart racing, she faced him. *"Ja?"*

He studied her and his eyes softened. "I know you wanted to put your plans on hold, but would it hurt to take a ride with me to see what other buildings might be available?" He paused. "For future reference."

"*Nay*, I suppose not." She missed spending time with him. Here was her chance.

"Will you come with me next week? Monday?"

She nodded. "Nine o'clock?"

"*Ja*, nine will be fine." He reached out to brush back a lock of hair that had escaped from beneath its pins. Her heart fluttered. "I'll come for you."

"Oll recht."

"Leah, don't you be canceling on me."

She blushed. This man had gone out of his way to help her, she had to remember that. "I'm sorry."

"Leah, I already said that there is nothing to be sorry for."

"I'll see you tomorrow then."

"Ja." Pleasure flickered in his gaze and was gone. He inclined his head, then left.

As she went inside, Leah realized that she was suddenly looking forward to the next two days. Tomorrow she'd see Henry at church service and then on Monday he'd be driving her around the county. She grinned. Despite her initial reservations, he was glad he'd come today and she was eager to see him again. What was it about Henry that he could so easily change her mind?

Sunday morning Henry and his family didn't come to church service. Disappointed and a bit miffed, Leah struggled to pay attention to Preacher Levi's sermon. Her thoughts went from anger to worry to fear as she began to wonder why Henry hadn't come. *Something must have happened.*

Directly after the service came to a close, she went to Isaac to ask if he'd heard from his friend.

"Nay," Isaac told her when she managed to find a moment alone with him. "He told me he'd be here."

"I'm worried," she admitted.

Isaac's gaze reflected her concern. "I'll stop by his *haus* later to see if he is *oll recht*."

Leah wanted to go, but didn't know if it was right for her to ask. Until she recalled the kindness Henry had shown her—first the day of the storm and then later with his offer to teach her about storekeeping. "May I come with you?"

"Ja," her cousin said without hesitation.

Later that afternoon, after the midday meal, Leah accompanied Isaac as he steered his buggy toward the Harry Yoder residence. Less than a half hour later, her cousin drove the vehicle into the Yoder yard, past the store and toward the house farther up the lane. There was a buggy parked near the house. Leah frowned. Had Henry simply changed his mind about coming today?

She and Isaac got out of the carriage and approached the house. They exchanged glances before Isaac knocked on the rear entrance door. They waited for someone to answer but when no one came, Isaac knocked hard on the wood with his fist.

"I don't think they're home," Leah said before Isaac could voice the same thought. "I hope nothing's bad happened."

Isaac's expression held concern. "Doesn't look like they went to a church service," he replied as he gestured toward the family buggy in the yard.

"Where could they have gone?"

"Maybe something happened with Henry's *vadder*."

"How can we find out?"

"Call the hospital?" Isaac gazed at the house with worry.

"Should we go to Whittier's Store?"

"Ja." her cousin urged. "We can use Bob's phone. He may have heard if anything bad happened."

Leah climbed into the passenger side while Isaac hopped into the driver's seat and picked up the reins. Her cousin urged his horse into a canter in the direction of Whittier's Store. It seemed ironic, somehow, that the first place they went after Henry's strange absence would be Whittier's Store, the scene of the criminal vandalism that had caused problems for Isaac when he'd come onto the property to find Henry and their English friends spray-painting the exterior of the building. That night the culprits had fled, leaving Isaac to take the blame.

Isaac pulled into the lot and parked. He got out, tied his horse to a hitching post and gestured for Leah to follow him as he entered into the store.

Bob Whittier arched his brows when he saw them. "Shouldn't you be at church?"

"Service is over. We were hoping to use your phone," Leah told him.

"Henry Yoder and his family were to attend service with us today, but we haven't seen nor heard from them. We checked the house. There is no one home, yet their buggy was in the yard. Have you heard anything?"

The look in Bob's face made Leah's stomach burn. "Yes, I'm afraid so. I'm in the ambulance corps. Yesterday I heard a call to the Yoder residence on my scanner. Someone was rushed to the hospital."

"Do you know who?" Isaac asked with concern.

"I'm sorry, I don't. We don't discuss names or conditions on the radio after the initial call."

Leah grew increasingly worried. She felt terrible. She'd been silently condemning him for not keeping his word, and he could be seriously hurt. "Which hospital?" she asked.

"Lancaster General."

She was familiar with the place. It was the same hospital her sister Meg had been in after she and Reuben Miller had suffered a buggy accident. "May we use your phone? I'll pay."

The man looked offended. "Feel free, but I'll not be taking your money under the circumstances."

She held his gaze a moment, then nodded. "Isaac?"

Her cousin took the hint. "Thank you. I'll make the call."

Leah hovered nearby and listened while Isaac spoke with someone on the other end of the line.

"I'm calling to see if Henry Yoder is there. I understand a family member was brought in by ambulance yesterday." Isaac paused to listen. "He is? Can you put me through to his room?...What?...Is there anyone in the family who I can talk with?...Fine. I'll wait." He met her gaze while he was on hold, his expression grim. "'Tis Henry who's in the hospital."

The burn in her stomach intensified as she waited for someone to come back on the line. Isaac frowned. "*Hallo?* Henry! Are you *oll recht*? They said it was you in the hospital! Oh, *ja*, that's right. Your father's given name is Henry, too." He listened quietly while Henry apparently told him what had occurred. "I'm sorry to hear that. Is it bad?" Her cousin exhaled sharply. "We'll keep Harry in our prayers." He paused. "Henry, Leah is here with me. *Ja*, I will."

He met her gaze and held out the phone receiver to her. "Henry wants to talk with you."

She swallowed hard as she moved closer and accepted the phone receiver. "Henry?" she greeted tentatively.

"Leah! I'm sorry. I know we made plans for tomorrow, but I won't be able to make it. My *dat* suffered another heart attack." He sounded choked up as he continued. "We don't know the extent of the damage yet, but it doesn't look good."

"Henry," she whispered, aching for him. "I'm sorry. Is there anything I can do?"

He grew quiet. It must have been only a few seconds, but it seemed much longer before he spoke again. "I wish…I could see you. I was looking forward to spending time with you tomorrow."

"We'll have time for that when your *vadder* is better."

A hesitation. "*Ja.* Plenty of time." She heard an odd strangled sound from his end of the line. "May I talk with Isaac again?" he asked.

"Ja." Feeling slightly hurt by his desire to get off the phone with her, Leah said, "I'll keep your *dat* and your *mam* and you in my prayers, Henry. Stay strong."

She heard warmth in his tone as he said, "*Danki.* I will."

Leah handed the phone to Isaac. After a quick glance at Bob, she stepped outside for some fresh air, hoping to calm herself. She wished she could do something to help him. She wanted to see him. Isaac came out of the store seconds later and eyed her with a knowing look. "Bob is calling someone to take us to the hospital."

She glanced at him with surprise. "Now?"

Her cousin nodded. "He's also going to get word to our families where we've gone."

He paused to gaze at her steadily. "You want to go, *ja*?"

Overcome with relief, she nodded. "I want to go," she admitted softly.

Isaac smiled. "'Tis *oll recht*, Leah. I understand how you feel. Henry's a *gut* man. You may think you know what happened that night, but you don't."

She knew he was referring to that night years ago when Whittier's Store had been vandalized. "And you still won't tell me," she said with resignation.

"*Nay*, I won't."

Bob Whittier stuck his head out the door. "Rick Martin is coming to take you to the hospital."

Leah turned to him with a smile. "Thank you."

"My pleasure. Please let Henry and his family know that I'm thinking about them."

She blinked, surprised by his request. "I will." Then Bob disappeared back into his store.

She faced her cousin. "He holds no ill will toward Henry—or you."

"*Nay*, he doesn't, and that tells you something about the situation, doesn't it?"

She gazed at him irritably without replying. At that moment, Rick Martin, an *Englisher* who often helped out members of their Amish community whenever they needed a ride, pulled up before them.

Leah greeted Rick as she got into the back while Isaac climbed into the front seat. As she stared out the car window during the ride to the hospital, she couldn't stop thinking about Henry. Would he be pleased to see her?

Chapter Nine

Henry sat in the chair next to the bed, gazing at his ill father, listening to the *beep, beep, beep* of the heart monitor. His *dat* looked pale. An IV drip was attached to his left arm and he lay as still as death. If it weren't for the rhythmic heart sound, he might have thought his father had died. He sensed movement on the other side of his parent's bed. He glanced over and saw his mother stir in her chair. She had fallen asleep and he hadn't the heart to wake her. They'd been at the hospital since late yesterday afternoon after his father had cried out and gripped his chest, and Henry had known that he'd suffered a second heart attack, this one much worse than the first one.

He rose from his seat and skirted the hospital bed, coming to stand at his mother's side. He placed a hand gently on her shoulder. "*Mam*, may I get you something to eat or drink?" he said softly. "You need to keep up your strength."

Mam released a shuddering sigh. "I could use a cup of tea."

Henry lightly squeezed his mother's shoulder. "I'll

get it and come right back." He hunkered down so that he could directly meet her gaze. "He's going to be fine."

He saw her swallow hard. "I hope so."

"He will," he insisted. He stood and smiled at her tenderly. "I'll be right back."

She acknowledged his comment with a nod, and he left the room and headed for the elevator. He, too, needed something to keep up his strength. Henry rode the elevator toward the lower level, where the cafeteria was located. He had a lot on his mind, with his father's illness. The elevator stopped and, without thought, he got off, only to realize that he had stepped out on the wrong floor.

"Henry!" a familiar male voice called, and he saw Isaac and Leah. He felt a punch of gladness in his chest.

He managed a smile as he approached and met them halfway. "'Tis *gut* to see you, Isaac." His gaze settled on Leah. His voice softened. "Leah. *Danki* for coming."

"Are you *oll recht*?" Leah asked with genuine concern.

Henry shrugged. "Better than my *dat*." He was tired, but seeing the two of them had raised his spirits.

"You look about ready to drop," Isaac commented. "Were you headed home?"

He shook his head, aware of Leah's study of him. "I'm going downstairs for something to eat."

"May we come with you?" Leah asked shyly.

His heart melted as he met her gaze. "I'd like that." She looked pretty in her Sunday-best royal blue dress with white prayer *kapp*, cape and apron. Her garment's blue fabric accentuated the blue of her eyes, making them shimmer.

"Is he doing any better?" Isaac asked as they stepped into the elevator.

"I don't know," Henry admitted. "The doctor hasn't given us an update." He ran a hand through his dark hair. He was exhausted and so was his mother. He needed food quickly to keep up his strength. Since they'd arrived, he hadn't left his father's bedside, but he knew that he and his mother couldn't continue without eating. It was bad enough that he'd barely slept.

"I'm sure you'll hear something soon," Isaac said encouragingly.

He was startled when Leah touched his arm. "Henry," she murmured, "is there anything we can do?" She quickly drew back when he halted and faced her. "We saw your buggy at the house. I can take care of your horses for you."

His heart fluttered, then beat harder. "You would do that for me?"

She looked puzzled. "Of course. You've been…" Her voice trailed off as she looked away as if embarrassed.

"That's a fine idea," Isaac said. "Henry, Leah will care for your horses until you get home."

Henry studied her, liking what he saw, grateful that she was willing to step in and help when he needed her. "I'd appreciate it, but our neighbor is seeing to them today." He felt something spark between him and Leah, an odd awareness that tightened his chest and made her blush and avert her gaze.

The elevator stopped. They got out and entered the cafeteria. "What would you like?" Henry asked. "Coffee and a sandwich? My treat." He was eager to show his appreciation of their visit.

"We ate before we came," Leah replied.

"A cup of tea? You're not going to allow me to eat alone?"

Amusement lit up her gaze, and he recalled the tea they enjoyed on the day of Alta Hershberger's visit to the store. "A cup of tea then."

"I'll have a soda," Isaac said. "But I'm paying, not you. Please, Henry, let me buy today."

His eyes stung and he blinked several times as he looked at his friend.

Isaac studied him thoughtfully. "Don't even think about paying me back."

Despite the circumstances, Henry laughed. "I'm glad you're here." He turned to Leah. "Both of you."

He ate his sandwich quickly while Leah drank her tea and Isaac his soda. When he was finished, Henry stood, eager to return to his father's room. "I have to get back."

"We'll come with you," Isaac said.

He was pleased when Isaac and Leah followed him into the elevator. He wasn't sure how many visitors his *dat* was allowed to have, but Henry decided that he would insist that Isaac and Leah stay if anyone tried to convince them to leave. He really wanted his friends with him—Isaac, his closest friend—and Leah, a woman who was quickly becoming to mean the world to him. His mother, he knew, would be happy for the distraction of their visit. He glanced toward his best friend who had insisted on carrying his mother's tea. Leah held a bag of chocolate-chip cookies that Isaac had insisted on buying while Henry carried the roast-turkey sandwich he'd decided his mother needed to eat.

The ride up in the elevator was made in silence. Henry stared at the lit floor numbers that flashed above the door. He felt Leah's gaze while they waited to reach the third floor. He glanced in her direction as the elevator eased to a stop. She blushed but didn't look away, and the tenderness in her expression made his breath hitch.

"Room 322," he said softly as he headed in the right direction. Henry grew worried as he neared the door until he peeked inside and saw his mother was still where he'd left her, seated in the chair by his father's bedside. He looked at the bed and was relieved to see that his father's eyes were open. His *dat* looked tired, but the fact that he was awake gave Henry hope.

"Dat!" he said with a grin. "You're awake. How are you feeling?"

"Tired but alive," his father grumbled, and Henry's grin widened.

"*Mam*, I've brought you a turkey sandwich…and a couple of friends have stopped by to say *hallo*." He turned as Isaac and Leah entered the room.

"Isaac!" his mother exclaimed. "'Tis *gut* to see you." She turned to her husband. "Harry, look who's come!"

To Henry's relief, a small smile settled on his father's lips. "Isaac," he said warmly. "Who's that with you? Is that Ellen?"

"*Nay*, Harry," Isaac said. "'Tis Leah, my cousin."

Leah smiled as she approached the man's bed. "I'm glad to see you're awake," she said.

"You're Arlin's daughter," his father said.

"*Ja*, second eldest." Her smile dimmed. "I'm sorry you're not feeling well."

"I'll live," the older man said. "At least, the doctor says so."

"Dat," Henry breathed with joy. "How bad is the damage?"

"There's some, but not as bad as we feared," his

mother said, answering for him, "and with a change in heart medication, he should do well."

"Thanks be to God," Henry said. He felt the tension in his shoulders drain away.

"He'll have to stay another couple of days," *Mam* said. "I want to stay but you should go home, *soohn*."

Henry shook his head. "I'm staying."

"But the horses..."

"I'll care for them," Leah said.

"Anything you need?" Isaac asked after a glance at the wall clock. "A change of clothes?"

"*Nay*, I grabbed some things before we left the house." He focused his gaze on Leah. "I'll send word when we're home."

She bobbed her head, then turned her attention to the man in the hospital bed. "Harry, I hope you feel better soon."

Henry watched her as she and Isaac left, overjoyed that she had come, wishing that he could have spent more time with her.

Just over a week later, Henry saw his father settled in a chair in their family's great room before he entered the kitchen to check on his mother. "*Mam*, would you like me to open the store today?"

His mother turned from the dishes in the sink. "*Ja*, I think I should stay here with your *dat*."

He inclined his head. "Is there anything you need?"

His *mam* smiled as she shook her head. "*Nay*. We'll be fine."

He saw a good opening to talk about an important matter. "I know that you and *Dat* never wanted a cell phone, but after what happened, don't you think it would be wise to have one? We can't always rely on our neighbors to get us help."

"I agree."

"*Dat* will argue against one."

"I'll talk with your *vadder.* Twice he's been in the hospital. I'll convince him that it's time."

"And 'tis *gut* for business." Henry grabbed a key from a wall peg. "I need to run an errand, but I'll open the store." He turned to leave.

"Henry."

He faced her. *"Ja?"*

"*Danki* for all you've done."

He shifted uncomfortably. "I've not done anything another son wouldn't do for his parents." His mother gave him an affectionate smile. He smiled back, then headed toward the door. He meant what he'd said. He loved his parents. They'd stood by him when things got tough. It was always right that he would do the same for them.

"You're a *gut* man, Henry."

He swallowed hard. "I've got to run, but I'll be back."

"Maybe you can look into buying us a cell phone," his mother said softly.

Henry grinned. "I can do that."

"A plain phone—nothing fancy."

He chuckled. "*Ja*, I'll find us a plain phone."

He left the house and drove his buggy to the Stoltzfus residence. He had promised to tell Leah when his father had come home. The doctor had released *Dat* later than either his mother or he had expected. *Dat* had a follow-up appointment soon. Henry would offer to take him, but he had a feeling that his mother would want to be the one to drive his father to make sure she received specific instructions on his care.

The day was unseasonably warm for a week into summer. It felt more like late in the season with the rise in temperature and humidity. Still Henry didn't mind. His father was home, and he was grateful that his parent was alive. And he was happy that he would soon see Leah. He hadn't been able to meet with her again last week, but she'd understood. It had been sweet of her and Isaac to visit and for Leah to care for the horses while they were gone.

The concern for him on Leah's face had warmed his heart. He spurred his horse into a canter in his eagerness to see her again. His decision to visit Leah first thing had come to him during the night. His time working in the store would be the perfect opportunity to resume her storekeeping lessons.

The Arlin Stoltzfus residence loomed ahead. A sudden case of nerves unsettled his stomach as he steered his horse onto the driveway and drove toward the house. He parked the buggy close to the barn and got out. Would Leah be pleased to see him? He swallowed against a suddenly dry throat as he approached the residence. He halted when he caught sight of someone at the clothesline in the backyard. The woman was young and blonde. Leah? Or Ellie?

He watched as she lifted a wet garment from the laundry basket near her feet before she pinned it to the line. *Leah.* He could tell it was her by the way she moved. He'd always been overly aware of Leah Stoltzfus.

He headed in her direction. "Leah!"

"Henry!" She eyed him shyly as he approached.

"My *dat* is home from the hospital."

"Is he doing well?"

He nodded. "We brought him home late yesterday."

She smiled. "I'm so glad." She held his gaze. "You must be relieved."

"*Ja*, his doctor is pleased with his recovery. 'Tis been a long few days."

Concern filled her blue eyes. "Are you *oll recht*?"

I am now. He was startled by how much he enjoyed being in her company. "I'm fine. I wanted to let you know that we were home. Thanks for taking care of our horses. I see that you fed them before we got up this morning." Her smile confirmed it. "I'll be working in the store this afternoon. Would you like to resume your lessons?" His heart accelerated at the prospect of spending time with her.

Her features filled with regret. "I would have liked to, but I have to houseclean with Ellie."

Henry felt something wither inside of him. "Just let me know when."

Leah tilted her head as she looked up at him. "We're not cleaning our *haus*, Henry. I'll be helping to clean for one of Ellie's English customers. This particular *haus* is huge and she needs it done quickly and efficiently before the owners get home from work."

Henry closed his eyes briefly. *Thanks be to God.* "Tomorrow then?"

"In the morning?"

"Ja." His heart filled with joy when she agreed. He reined in his happiness. Fortunately, Leah didn't appear to notice his eagerness to work with her again. "I can come for you." He paused. "If you want, we can check out a location first before we head to the store."

She hesitated. "Are you sure you can get away?"

"*Ja, Mam* wants to open and work for an hour or two. *Dat* is going to sit and watch her." He shifted a few feet closer. "Leah—"

She pinned her father's shirt to the line. *"Ja?"*

"Danki."

She faced him, her brow furrowed. "For?"

"Coming to see us. For checking on the horses. It was *gut* to see you—and Isaac," he added quickly. "It had been a difficult day. Your visit cheered up not only me but *Mam* and *Dat*, too."

She beamed at him, and he felt her smile radiate over him like a bright burst of much-needed sunshine. "I'm glad we could come."

Silence reigned and the moment grew awkward. "I should go," he said. "I know you have things to do, and I need to get back and open the store." He turned to leave.

"Henry."

He swung back.

"I'll see you tomorrow."

"Nine o'clock." He held her gaze a moment longer before he turned and headed back to his buggy, aware that she had gone back to work and wasn't watching him as he would have liked. He sighed. His feelings were one-sided. Still, he had tomorrow to look forward to. Once he opened the store, he would see what he could do to prepare for Leah's next lesson. He climbed into his vehicle, grabbed the reins and, with a flick of the leathers, drove toward the road. Henry glanced over his shoulder and felt an infusion of warmth when he saw Leah, with the empty basket in her arms, staring in his direction as he departed. He grinned with satisfaction.

* * *

"Can I get you anything?" Henry asked after he'd helped to see his father settled in a chair by the front counter in the store. His parents had decided to spend the day rather than just the morning.

"We are fine, Henry," *Mam* assured him.

"We have a store filled with anything we could possibly need," his father added.

"Are you feeling well, *Dat*?"

"I'm fine, *soohn*, but your *mudder* insists that I stay in this chair. I told her I would sit today, but that tomorrow would be a different story. I have plenty of energy with this new medicine, and I need to exercise." He glanced at his wife. "Doctor's orders."

Henry laughed. "I'll be back to relieve you a little later."

"No need. We'll manage," his mother said. "Take some time for yourself today. You've earned it."

Satisfied that his parents were happy to be left alone for the day, Henry got into his buggy and drove to pick up Leah.

Leah was waiting for him as he pulled into the yard. She smiled as she approached. "*Hallo*, Henry."

"Leah." He felt his breath quicken at the sight of her. He helped her into his buggy, then climbed in. He studied her with a smile. "*Mam's* working all day. If you still want to come, I thought we'd ride around and see if we see anything interesting." He paused. "Do you want to go or stay since we can't use the store?"

"'Tis too nice of a day to be inside," she replied. "I'd like to go."

Henry experienced a rush of pleasure.

The afternoon flew by quickly as they drove through

the area, looking for potential locations for her craft shop. They stopped for lunch in a local diner before they continued their search. They didn't see any building worth looking at, but Leah didn't seem to mind, and Henry was glad. He was happy to simply enjoy her company as they discussed the area, the sights and the neighbors in their community. All too soon for Henry, it was time to take Leah home.

"I enjoyed our ride," Leah said after he'd hurried around to help her step down from his vehicle.

"I did, too," Henry admitted huskily. "I'm sorry we didn't find anything worth consideration. I should have gone out ahead of time to look for places to show you."

"*Nay*, Henry. There is no rush. Remember, I wanted to put my plans on hold. It was fun searching the area, but I'm not worried. Eventually, when I'm ready, I'll find something."

He nodded. "When can I see you again?" He stiffened when he realized what he'd said.

"Sunday?" she said.

He relaxed when he saw the teasing twinkle in her blue eyes. "*Ja*, no doubt." He smiled. "Service is at Abram Peachy's?"

"It is."

"I'll see you then." He climbed into his buggy and, with a wave, left. He'd wanted nothing more than to stay and talk with Leah longer, but he was afraid that she'd discover that he had deep feelings for her…and the last thing he wanted to do was to scare her away.

He'd steered his horse about a mile down the road when a car came up from behind him and slowed. Henry glanced over and sighed. *Not again.*

"Henry," a male voice sang with a cruel expression.

"Whatcha doing?" The *Englisher* pulled his car off the road, and Henry had no other choice but to face him.

"Brad," he greeted pleasantly. "We meet again. What do you want?" Why wouldn't man leave him alone?

The man looked amused. "I thought we'd visit awhile."

Henry stared at him calmly, but inside his heart started to hammer hard. The man was nothing but trouble. Years before, Isaac and he had been too young and inexperienced to recognize Brad for the cruel bully he was. If they had, they would have avoided Brad and his English friends instead of befriending them. Unfortunately, he and Brad Smith shared a past, and there was nothing Henry could do about it, except refuse to let the man intimidate him a second time.

Chapter Ten

Sunday morning Leah sat in the back of the family buggy with her sisters. She had yet to ask her parents about her adoption again. Partly because they were talking again, and she didn't want to do anything that would make things difficult and tense between her and Missy and Arlin. After meeting Jess in the barn, she realized how lucky she was to have adoptive parents who'd cared for her. As her father steered the buggy toward the Abram Peachy residence, where church service would be held, Leah wondered how Jess was faring. She'd seen no evidence of the girl's return. She sighed. She hoped Jess was all right. She was worried about her. She should have done more and offered the girl a safe haven, perhaps consulted with one of the church elders.

I don't know her situation, but it doesn't mean I couldn't have done more for her. She sighed. Jess would have run away as fast as she could if Leah had tried to do anything more. Leah prayed that the girl would return if she was in trouble.

She got the sudden urge to see Henry. She had enjoyed her outing with him. She reminded herself to be cautious with her heart. The Henry Yoder she was beginning to know wasn't the kind of man who would hurt anyone intentionally. She'd trusted him enough to confide in him. It might have been impulsive to tell him the secret of her adoption, but she didn't regret talking with him.

The Yoders would be attending today's service. Leah recognized the rush of anticipation as pleasure at the thought of spending time with him.

Leah felt butterflies in her stomach as her father turned onto Abram Peachy's property.

After *Dat* parked their buggy, she scrambled out of the vehicle after her sisters and waved to her cousin Isaac and his wife, Ellen. With the cake she'd baked in her arms, she approached them. "*Hallo*, cousins."

Ellen beamed at her. "Leah, 'tis wonderful to see you. You're looking well."

"You are, too," Leah replied with a smile. She glanced past the couple for any sign of Henry.

"Looking for someone, Leah?" Isaac said with amusement.

She raised her eyebrows and answered truthfully. "I'm looking for Henry. I need to talk with him."

Her honesty surprised her cousin. His teasing twinkle vanished. "He's not here yet. I talked with him yesterday and he said his parents were coming, too."

"I'll look for him after service." She held up her plate. "I need to put this cake inside."

The benches in Abram Peachy's great room were set up in sections, one section for women and children and the others for the men and older boys. Abram was a church elder and deacon. The family of his wife,

Charlotte King Peachy, were neighbors of her aunt Katie and uncle Samuel.

There was no sign of Henry as she took a seat in the women's section of the congregation. Leah watched as her sisters and their husbands came in and sat down. Nell grinned as she sat next to her, and Leah, pleased to see her sister, returned her grin. Sarah, her cousin Jedidiah's wife, grabbed a seat on the bench directly in front of them with her two children. Her cousin Noah's wife, Rachel, murmured a greeting as she and her daughter, Susanna, sat on Leah's other side.

Leah leaned over to ruffle Susanna's hair before she sat back. Her pulse rate changed as Henry and his parents entered the room. Her gaze locked with Henry's. She nodded a greeting with the hope that he'd approach her after the service.

Preacher Levi Stoltzfus entered the pulpit area. Everyone stood, opened the *Ausbund*, the book of hymns, and began to sing. Afterward, Levi began to speak. Everyone was silent as they listened, including the youngest members of their Amish community. Deacon Abram rose and said a few words. The service was interspersed with hymns and sermons until church ended and everyone stood to leave the room. The men grabbed benches to bring outside to use as seats for the midday meal. The women headed toward the kitchen to get the food. Leah pitched in to help take out cold food dishes and paper plates with plastic utensils.

The weather was perfect for eating outside. The men set the benches near tables made from plywood laid across wooden sawhorses. A separate table was created to hold food. Leah went back and forth to the house until all the family food donations had been put out for the community. To drink, there were pitchers of iced tea and lemonade and several bottles of soda. Their young children had the choice of milk or juice.

The women waited until the men were seated before they served them. The conversation at the table was of crops, animals, weather and local businesses. Henry sat beside his father, who looked well despite his recent hospital stay. Margaret fixed a plate of food for her husband and son before she went to get her own meal. During the colder months, when forced to eat inside, the men would eat first, then give their seats to their women and children. Leah loved this time of year best. The good weather allowed for enough table room for families to eat together.

She glanced toward her adoptive mother and felt a catch in her throat. This woman had mothered her since she was a baby. Leah knew that she had no reason to complain. Missy might not be her birth mother, but she had raised and loved her. If it wasn't for her deep-seated desire to know the truth—no matter how painful—Leah would have allowed the matter of her adoption to rest. Were her parents afraid that the truth would hurt more than help her?

Nell and Meg were filling plates for themselves and their husbands when Leah approached. "Are you certain you have enough to eat?" she teased as she grabbed a paper plate for herself.

Meg stared at the overfilled plate she'd fixed for Peter. She looked amused when she met Leah's gaze. "Too much?"

Nell considered the plate Meg held carefully. "I don't know. Maybe you should add a piece of cake."

"Peter needs a separate plate for dessert."

Leah chuckled. "Meg, 'tis *gut* to see you," she said sincerely. "You, too, Nell. I've missed you both. Everything seems different now that you're married and out of the *haus*."

"What about you?" Meg asked. "No beau or potential husband?"

"As if I could pick and choose whom to marry," Leah said with a sigh.

"Are you *oll recht*, Leah?" Nell studied her with concern.

"Ja." Leah managed a smile. "Trying to decide on the chocolate cake or the vanilla cream pie for dessert."

She followed her sisters to their family table. As she approached, she and her *dat* exchanged looks. She smiled shyly as she took the seat directly across from him. "A beautiful day for a meal outside. I'm glad to be here," she murmured and was rewarded with the look of pleasure in her mother's expression.

"Leah."

She recognized the male voice immediately. She faced him with a smile. "Henry."

"When you're done, do you have a minute to talk?"

She felt a burning in her stomach at his unreadable expression. "*Ja.* Just give me a few minutes."

He appeared serious as he inclined his head. "I'll be with my *eldre* until you're ready."

When she faced them, she saw her family's curiosity. "Business," she explained, although she was afraid that it wasn't business he wanted to discuss with her.

She finished her meal, then threw away her trash. Henry was seated with his parents in the next row of tables. She hesitated before approaching. Had something happened since they last saw each other? Why was she so worried?

Because I like him—maybe too much. She started toward the table. Henry saw her and stood, murmured something to his parents and came to meet her.

"You wanted to talk with me?" she asked, her heart thumping hard. His features were stiff, almost angry. She didn't understand, because that wasn't the Henry she knew. That man had only ever been kind to her.

"Let's walk this way," he said abruptly, then started toward the road before making a right onto the front farm field of Abram Peachy's property.

Leah was aware that he purposely kept his distance as they walked side by side. It was as if they'd never worked together or become friends. *Friends.* Was he worried that she saw him as more than a friend? She was attracted to him, but she'd been polite and she hoped she'd done nothing to make him think that their working relationship was anything other than friendship. So she missed him when she wasn't with him. She'd given him a glimpse of her vulnerable side and questioned the wisdom of it since she'd cried and he'd tried to make her feel better. And he'd offered her good advice. A knot of pain formed in her chest. Yes, she longed for more than friendship from Henry Yoder, but she had no plans for telling him.

Her throat tightened and he remained tensely silent. Unable to stand it any longer, she stopped and face him. "Henry." She felt him stiffen as he halted and met her gaze. "Have I done something to offend you?"

"Nay," he said.

"Then what?" Panic set in. Was Henry ill? What could have happened to make him study her so seriously? She stared into his blue eyes and knew. "You don't want to help me anymore."

His expression softened. "I can't work with you," he said huskily. "Not right now."

She blanched. "I see."

"I'm going to be busy over the next couple of weeks, and I needed to let you know. To explain."

"I understand." But she didn't and turned so he couldn't see her tears.

He gently touched her arm, and she closed her eyes with longing and a world of hurt. "Leah," he whispered. "I'm sorry."

She hardened her heart and faced him defiantly. "I've heard no explanation."

He opened his mouth, then closed it. "You have a lot on your mind with Missy and Arlin, and I have to worry about my *vadder*."

Her insides softened at the mention of his father. "Is Harry *oll recht*? He seems well enough."

He refused to meet her gaze. "He's been having a *gut* week, but I worry that he'll suffer a relapse."

Leah narrowed her eyes. "I see." The sudden impression that he wasn't telling the whole truth struck her hard, because she'd come to expect better from him.

Harry Yoder wasn't the reason that Henry no longer wanted to work with her. Unless it was because he'd had enough of her and wanted to ease back from their friendship until it was over.

She nearly gasped at the pain. She blinked rapidly and was able to control her tears.

"Leah."

She managed to smile. "I understand, Henry. I do." She drew a calming breath. "*Danki* for all that you've taught me. You're a great teacher." She glanced back toward the table area where her family and friends would be enjoying dessert. "We should head back. I want a piece of chocolate cake before it's gone."

She felt his stare but she didn't look at him until, after a long silent moment, he seemed to demand it of her. She gazed up to see a something like regret flicker in his blue eyes. "I wouldn't mind a slice myself," he said. His smile was slight, missing his usual gorgeous good humor.

"Then we'd better hurry. Noah is here, and he's bound to jump in and eat our share if we don't claim it."

Tension hung between as they approached the community area. Leah immediately walked to the dessert table and picked up a plate. Aware that Henry had left her, she turned to see that he'd rejoined his family. She fought back tears as she cut a generous piece of chocolate cake. For once, her cousin Noah hadn't returned for more. Her dessert plate blurred as she headed slowly toward her family's table. Until Henry stepped into her path and blocked her. She gaped at him. "May I sit with you?" he asked.

She stared at him in shock and couldn't help the sudden rising surge of hope. Maybe he liked her a little. She nodded, and he led her to an empty table, vacated by her cousins, who were playing ball on the back lawn. Without looking at him, Leah slid her legs under the table as she sat down.

Henry didn't say a word but seemed more at ease. "The cake looks delicious," he finally said, drawing her glance.

Her heart beat wildly as she met his gaze. "I like chocolate."

His lips curved crookedly. “Me, too.” He’d taken a couple of brownies and a small piece of the chocolate cake Leah had baked yesterday. Holding her gaze captive, he didn’t look away. “Leah,” he began. He shifted uncomfortably. “I…like you.”

Her pulse raced. “I like you, too,” she admitted softly.

He looked away. “I don’t know what to do,” he murmured.

She wrinkled her brow. “I don’t understand.”

He sighed. “I can’t spend time with you, but I’d like to.”

Leah was surprised to see real regret in his expression. “Henry—”

“I want to see you, Leah, but… I can’t explain why I can’t.” She saw herself mirrored in his blue eyes. “But I’d like to spend today with you.”

Henry gazed at the woman before him and experienced a pain so intense in the region of his heart that it nearly stole his breath. He wanted nothing more than to be with Leah, but how could he after Brad’s threats to harm anyone he cared about? The *Englisher* was angry. He’d had nothing to do with the man’s time in jail, but Brad was determined to blame someone for his troubles—and unfortunately, he’d chosen Henry. If only Isaac and he had stayed away from the *Englisher*. Newly on *rumspringa*, they’d become caught up in the excitement of having English friends. Until they discovered, after it was too late, that Brad had no conscience. The man had enjoyed defacing Whittier’s Store and taken great pleasure when Henry had become upset and tried to stop him. Yesterday wasn’t the first time that Brad had threatened his family and friends. Henry hadn’t done the crime, but it had felt as if he had, for he was ashamed that he hadn't been brave enough to come forward with the truth—even after Isaac was blamed—because he'd been afraid of the *Englisher.*

Later, when Brad was in jail and no longer a threat, Henry had finally confessed. A visit by Isaac's sweetheart, Ellen Mast, had influenced his decision to come forward. His silence had destroyed his best friend's reputation. Isaac hadn't denied the wrongdoing to protect him, and Henry had suffered with guilt, even after he'd stood up before his church district and told the truth. Although forgiven, Henry hadn't been able to forgive himself until recently, when Leah's forgiveness had soothed his guilt-ridden soul. Since then, he had discovered his life was a blessing while he enjoyed every moment with Leah Stoltzfus.

Now, with Brad's recent threats hanging over his head, Henry had no choice but to distance himself from her for her protection when all he wanted to do was to hang on tight. *Lord, please help me to let her go to keep her safe.*

Brad mustn't learn about his friendship with Leah. If he didn't, things would be fine. Henry wanted the gift of today and then he'd step away. He'd find a way to ease back without hurting her. The distance would devastate him, for he would suffer forever with his longing for her. If he could figure out a way to eliminate the threat one day, he'd seek Leah's forgiveness and beg her to take him back.

"Leah?" He shifted as he stared at her. "You haven't answered me. May I spend the rest of the day with you?"

Dark lashes blinked across bright blue eyes as she bobbed her head. "Would you like more dessert?" she asked.

He grinned. "I wouldn't mind. You?"

Her lips curved in a teasing smile. "Maybe."

As he gazed at her, he knew that he wouldn't be able to stay away from her. As long as he could have her and keep her safe. They could spend Sundays together, he thought. He doubted Brad would seek him out on church or Visiting Days. Henry became overwhelmed with a sudden rush of warmth and tenderness, laced with extreme excitement, that he might not have to keep his distance from Leah on Sundays.

He watched as she cut two pieces of apple pie, He had to find a way to keep Leah in his life. Was Brad Smith really a threat? If he hurt anyone, the *Englisher* would end up in jail again, the last place Brad wanted to be.

Overjoyed, Henry beamed at Leah with warmth as she handed him his plate. "*Danki*, Leah." He was surprised when she blushed. Her pink cheeks and shy smile made his heart pound and fill up with hope. He sent up a silent prayer, asking the Lord for Leah and him to have a future together, that Leah would love him as he loved her. *Please, Lord.* He wouldn't tell her of his love, not until he knew if she shared his feelings. He would enjoy her company and enjoy their growing friendship, and he'd continue to pray that their relationship would become something more…and permanent.

Chapter Eleven

Henry was stocking the shelves with merchandise when he heard the bell on the entrance door. He glanced over and was pleasantly surprised to see Leah Stoltzfus.

"*Hallo*, Henry," she greeted.

His pulse rate shot up as she smiled at him warmly. "Leah. I didn't expect to see you today." She looked pretty in a lavender dress with matching cape and apron. Her white prayer *kapp* covered most of her blond hair without a strand out of place.

She held up a grocery list. "*Mam* needed a few items, so I offered to shop for her." She approached, and he watched her with no small amount of interest.

"Anything I can help with?" he asked softly.

Leah froze as she came within a few feet of him, as if she'd suddenly sensed something strong between them. "*Nay*, the list isn't too long." She turned away quickly, apparently eager to put distance between them.

He rushed after her, gently grabbed hold of her arm. "Leah."

She stiffened but met his gaze. He smiled to assure her that he was still the same man who'd taught her the basics of bookkeeping and storekeeping—her friend. "Would you like a cup of tea?"

The offer drew a reluctant smile. "Black tea with sugar? Lots of sugar?"

"If you'd like." He grinned. The awkwardness had dissipated. "I'll put on the hot water."

"I'll wander around the store while I wait."

Henry nodded and went behind the counter to brew the tea while he prayed that the easy camaraderie between them would remain and Leah would stay to visit for a while. When the tea was ready, he joined her on the other side of the counter with the two cups. "Here you are."

She accepted the cup with a murmur of thanks. "Your *mam* took the day off?"

His stomach lurched as he swallowed a sip of tea. "She took *Dat* for his follow-up doctor's appointment." Had she been disappointed to find him here instead of his mother? "How long is your *mudder's* list?"

"Not too long." She pulled the list from where she'd tucked it beneath the waistband of her apron and glanced over it. "Eight items."

"Are you sure you don't want me to help?" he asked with the hope that she'd say that she was in no hurry to shop and leave.

"*Danki*, but *nay*. I'll find them when I'm ready." Her blue eyes regarded him with a twinkle. "I'm enjoying my tea. I'm in no rush to check out."

Thank You, Lord, Henry thought.

Suddenly she frowned. "I don't mean to keep you from working."

"Leah," he said quietly, "I'm not worried about the store. I'd much rather spend this time with you." He eyed her carefully and was rewarded when she blushed. Did she feel it, too—the attraction, the camaraderie and warmth? He was thoughtful. "How about a cookie to go with your tea?"

"Chocolate?"

"If you'd like." He liked how her blue eyes shimmered with good humor.

She suddenly looked uncertain. "*Nay*, but *danki*. I should finish *Mam's* shopping and get home."

Her reluctance warmed his heart. "Will you…shop again?"

Leah grinned. "*Ja*, I like shopping here."

He couldn't help but grin back at her. He walked with her through the store, despite her initial refusal of his help, and worked with her to collect the items she needed. He followed her back to the counter where he rang up her merchandise, mostly food and bakery items. He grabbed a wrapped chocolate-chip cookie and put it in her bag. "For you." He eyed her shyly, hoping that she wouldn't refuse the treat. "For later, when you're hungry."

She chuckled. "I love chocolate-chip cookies."

His chest swelled with love. He then walked with her to the door and to her buggy. "How are things going with your parents? Have they told you anything about your adoption?"

"Nay," she confessed with a sadness that made him regret bringing up the painful topic.

"I'm sorry."

"Don't be. You've been…"

He arched an eyebrow.

"…helpful," she ended with a teasing twinkle that caused him to laugh out loud.

If she could laugh about it, he thought, maybe things would get better for her.

He helped her into her buggy. "I'll see you Sunday at the William Masts'." The family would be hosting Visiting Sunday for family and a few friends, including Henry and his parents.

Leah smiled, looking flushed, as she agreed before she steered her horse out of the parking lot.

Henry had turned back to the store when he heard a car engine roar up from behind him. He spun and felt the drop in his stomach when he recognized the driver.

The *Englisher* rolled down the side window. "Henry."

"What do you want now, Brad?" He was glad that Leah had left. If she had been here… Henry felt a chill.

"Just thought I'd stop for a quick chat with an old *friend*."

"I can't stay to talk with you. I've got work to do."

Anger flashed across the *Englisher's* blunt features. He drew a sharp breath. "Guess we all got to make a living, huh?"

Henry nodded, unwilling to look away, because he didn't trust him.

"Can't stay, either. Mom's making me my favorite dinner."

"That's nice." He remembered how much the man's mother had favored her son over her daughter. Isaac had told him how Brad's sister, Nancy, had run away from home to seek refuge from her abusive brother, abuse that their mother refused to believe had occurred. Isaac had taken the girl to Abram Peachy, their deacon, who had made sure Nancy had a safe haven in a new home.

With a wave and a nasty snicker, Brad drove his car out of the lot. Henry had never been so happy to see him leave. *Please, Lord, keep Leah safe. And please protect my family and friends from Brad Smith.*

Henry woke in the middle of the night, wondering how he could help Leah find out about the circumstances of her adoption and what he could do to ensure that Brad Smith no longer had the power to disrupt the life of anyone he cared about. Missy Stoltzfus's parents lived in Ohio. He could visit them and find out what they knew. Did they know anything about Leah's birth parents?

He'd leave on Monday after Visiting Day. He could hire a driver or take the bus, then return as soon as he could. Leah wanted to know who her birth parents were. He would help her discover the truth. And while he was at it, he'd figure out a way to get Brad Smith out of his life once and for all. With a decision made, Henry exhaled softly and felt his eyelids droop closed.

Sunday couldn't come fast enough for Leah, who was eager to see Henry again. She had no reason to visit the store again. Her mother didn't need supplies, and she didn't want to appear forward and stop by simply to say *hallo*. Visiting Sunday was at William and Josie Mast's house, her cousin Isaac's in-laws. Upon arrival, Leah saw the Lapp clan in the yard with the women setting up for breakfast. She climbed down from the carriage with her egg casserole and looked for Henry. Her breath caught when she spied him chatting with Abram Peachy's eldest daughter, Mary Elizabeth. She experienced a sharp pain in her chest as he laughed at something the young woman had said. Then, as if sensing that she was there, he looked her way, excused himself quickly and hurried in her direction.

He grinned as he reached her. "Leah!" His look of pleasure filled her with happiness. "May I carry your dish for you?"

She shook her head as she beamed at him. "*Danki*, I can manage. I'm only taking it as far as there." She gestured toward the outside food table. She was surprised to see his cheeks redden with embarrassment. Henry was handsome and adorable, and her love-stricken heart started to pound hard. "'Tis egg casserole. Do you like egg casserole?" she asked in an attempt to get past the awkward moment.

He nodded. "Love it. Especially if it has cheese in it."

Leah affected a frown. "Mine doesn't have cheese."

Henry blinked as if he didn't know how to reply. "I like it without cheese."

She laughed. "I'm teasing you, Henry. *Ja*, it has cheese. What would an egg casserole be without lots of cheddar cheese?"

His face fell. "Oh, cheddar."

"You don't like cheddar." She was disappointed.

He burst out laughing. "Of course I like cheddar cheese." He eyed her with amusement. "I can tease, too."

As they grinned at each other, Leah felt her insides warm with affection. "Let me set this down."

To her surprise, he followed her. She didn't mind. There was something about being in his company that thrilled her. As she slid him a quick glance, she remembered how she had once regarded him and wondered how she could have ever thought ill of him. So he'd made a mistake. Everyone did at one time or another. And she knew Henry was genuinely sorry for his.

"Would you like to take a walk?" he asked, drawing her gaze.

"We haven't had breakfast." Still, she wanted to go now, even if it would seem odd if they disappeared without eating.

"After we eat then?" His blue eyes seemed to plead.

She nodded, moved by the fond look in his expression. "After breakfast," she agreed.

The day already showed signs of being Leah's best day ever. She ate breakfast with her family, whose table was next to Henry's so she and he basically sat side by side, and she loved every minute. A warning rose in her mind to protect her heart; she ignored it, as she already loved Henry and there was nothing she could do about it. She didn't tell him—and wouldn't—because while they were friends who clearly enjoyed each other's company, it was too soon for love. *Although I've known him for many years.* She'd thought she'd be spending her life with only her craft shop for company. She was scared to hope for marriage. Even her adoptive parents hadn't expected it of her. Did they know something about her, something horrible, that would prevent her from having a husband and children? She gasped. Maybe she couldn't have children!

Ellie, Charlie and Nell laughed at something James Pierce, Nell's husband, said. Leah saw a small smile curve her father's lips, and she realized how much she missed their close relationship. Aware of her gaze, he looked at her, and she fought back tears as she gave him a genuine smile. Something shifted in his expression, and she clearly saw his love and affection for her—his daughter. Her mother said something to him, and he turned to her. Leah inhaled sharply and wondered why she'd fought so hard to learn the truth about her birth parents. Did it matter who they were when she had a family who loved her? Her sisters didn't know the circumstances of her birth. What would they say if they knew?

She felt a warm hand entwine fingers with hers below the table. She shot Henry a glance to see his compassion and warmth…and an emotion she couldn't read.

Henry bent close and whispered in her ear, "We've eaten. Ready for our walk?"

Leah nodded. She rose with her used paper plate in hand and wandered to the trash can to throw it out. Some of her Lapp cousins had already risen and chatted nearby. She smiled at them and meandered toward the barn. She walked to the back of the building and waited for Henry to come. It seemed the best way to go for a walk without raising eyebrows. She didn't have long to wait. Henry approached from the other side of the barn and would have frightened her by his approach, except that she sensed him coming.

She turned as he rounded the corner. "Henry."

He regarded her warmly. "*Danki* for coming. We won't go far."

Henry led the way and headed to the back of Abram Peachy's property. "I don't think anyone saw me leave." Leah halted. "I'm sorry. I didn't think…"

"Leah," he said as he reached for her hand. "I wanted this time alone with you. 'Tis no one's business if we want to walk together."

She swallowed hard, disappointed.

"Not that I would care if everyone knew," he added, brightening her mood.

"You wouldn't?" she whispered.

In answer, he entwined his fingers with hers and gave them a little squeeze. "You're beautiful."

She blushed. "Henry."

"I mean it, Leah. I've always thought you so."

Leah stopped and faced him, eager to read his expression. She could tell that he told her the truth, and the knowledge startled as much as pleased her. "I don't know what to say."

He regarded her silently, his blue eyes filled with warmth and caring. "Then don't say anything. Let's walk."

And so they did. They started out in silence and soon relaxed enough to have a conversation about what they saw. The colorful array of summer wildflowers reminded them that the season was upon them. With Henry by her side, Leah appreciated the varied colored blossoms in white, yellow, purple and gold. The sun felt warm on her face and a light breeze caressed her skin, but it was the touch of Henry's hand against hers that gave her the most pleasure.

Neither spoke, as if the company of each other was enough. Time seemed to stand still until Leah realized how long they'd been gone and became afraid that someone would look for them.

"We should get back." She didn't want to end or ruin the moment but knew it was past time. She caught him studying her. "What?"

Henry shook his head. "You're right. We should get back." He, too, seemed reluctant to leave, which gave her hope.

As they walked back, Henry released her hand, but he continually brushed shoulders with her. Once they reached the barn, he stopped, gently grasped her arms and turned her to face him. “I enjoyed our walk.”

She inclined her head. “Me, too.”

“It will be lunchtime before we know it.”

“Ja.”

“I have to leave soon after lunch,” he said as they continued. “*Dat* still gets tired.”

Silently Leah continued on.

“Leah.”

She halted and met his gaze.

“I want to help you. May I?”

She frowned. “I don’t understand.”

“To learn the truth about your parents.”

“I’m fine, Henry. I’m letting it go.” She would try to, at least. She wanted to forget about the circumstances of her birth. And she would. She firmed her lips. “Henry, do you think there is a reason they won’t tell me? Like something bad about my real parents?”

He furrowed his brows. “Why would you think that?”

“Because my parents have never encouraged me to marry like they have my sisters.”

He shook his head. “I doubt that, Leah. They might have been more careful of you because they wanted you to choose for yourself.”

“But if they considered me their *dochter*, wouldn’t they treat me the same?”

Henry seemed to give the matter some thought. “There is nothing wrong with you,” he said. “Arlin and Missy may love you too much to push. Maybe they were afraid that you would be upset with them if they did.”

Leah stared at him. “Why would I be upset?”

His lips curved up slightly. “If they’d urged you to

find a husband before your younger sisters were allowed to wed, how would that make you feel?"

She blinked. "I don't know."

"There is nothing wrong with you, Leah Stoltzfus." He caught her hand, gave it a squeeze before releasing it.

At the barn, Henry and she parted ways, each returning the way they'd come—from opposite sides of the building. As she headed toward the gathering, Leah saw Ellie wave at her and she waved back. Henry was nowhere in sight as she joined her sister and went into the house with her to bring out food. Ellie didn't say a word about the length of time she and Henry had been gone and she was grateful for her sister's apparent lack of interest. It was only as the two of them left the house with plates in hand that Ellie turned to her with a secretive smile.

"So how was your walk with Henry Yoder?"

Leah gasped.

"That *gut*, *ja*?" Ellie laughed.

"Does everyone know?"

"Not everyone," her sister said. "Just Isaac, Ellen and me noticed."

"You won't say anything?"

Ellie regarded her worriedly. "Why not?"

"I don't know if it means anything. Henry has been teaching me about storekeeping, and—"

"Storekeeping?" Ellie chuckled. "Leah, that man doesn't look like he has storekeeping on his mind when he looks at you."

Chapter Twelve

Henry put his small suitcase into the car waiting in the yard. "I'll be back in a day or so," he told his parents.

"Check out that vendor while you're there, *ja*?" his *mam* said.

"I will." He'd decided the trip to Ohio could be used for three purposes—to visit the company they often ordered merchandise from, to speak with Leah's adoptive grandparents and to figure out what to do about his ongoing problem with Brad Smith. He'd be staying with his sister, an added bonus. He'd called the phone she used to take calls and asked if he could stay, then left the store's new cell phone number. Less than an hour later, Ruth had called back and told him she'd be pleased to have him stay with her.

He turned to his father. "*Dat*, take care and don't overdo it," he said softly.

Harry Yoder grimaced. "I'm fine."

"I know you are, but I feel better saying it to you with the hope that you'll actually take heed."

His *dat* chuckled. "I'm getting stronger every day, enough to keep your *mudder* company in the store."

I can live with that. "I'll see you soon. Anything you'd like me to bring back?"

"Your sister and her family?" his mother said with a wry smile. Her expression sobered. "You've got the quilt I made for her?"

"Have it."

"And the cookies I baked?"

"Have those, too, *Mam.*" He reached out and hugged his mother. To his surprise, she pulled him in tight. When she released him, he met his father's gaze. "Bye, *Dat.*"

More reserved than his wife, his father dipped his head in acknowledgment. "I'll call the cell when I get there, so you won't worry," Henry said.

He climbed into the front seat of the car. He knew the hired driver and figured he'd appreciate the company. He lifted a hand to wave to his parents as Timothy Trader drove out of the yard. Henry thought about what might lie ahead and realized that he already missed Leah more than he'd ever dreamed possible.

Leah went into the barn to feed the animals. She heard barking and decided to visit briefly with Jeremiah, their new puppy, before continuing with her chores. The first thing she noticed as she entered the stall was that someone had fed Jeremiah and filled his water bowl. She frowned. Her father hadn't been out to the barn yet, and she knew that her mother and sisters hadn't stepped outside. *Had Jess come back last night to sleep?*

She stared at the tamped straw as she bent to ruffle Jeremiah's fur. An idea came to her on how to help Jess if she came back, and it involved leaving food in a place that only the girl could find. Leah smiled as she took care of the other animals.

When she was done, Leah headed to the house. She froze at the sight of a large commercial van with a huge circular object on the roof. Her mother and father were in the yard, talking with two men who stood beside the vehicle.

One man spied her. "Is that her? Is that *his* daughter?"

"That is Leah and she is *our* daughter," she heard her father said tightly. "One of five." She quickly approached to stand by her parents.

"Leah, go into the *haus*," her father ordered.

Her heart beat wildly in her throat as she immediately obeyed.

"You need to leave," she heard her father say. "Ours is a quiet community. You have no right to be here. You don't belong, and I don't know where you got your information, but our daughters are ours—and no one else's."

She entered the kitchen and saw her two sisters at the window. "What's happening?" Leah suspected the men were here to talk with the adopted daughter of Arlin and Missy Stoltzfus. Her.

"I don't know. *Dat* told us to stay in the *haus*."

Leah joined them at the window. *Dat* and *Mam* were coming inside. The men hadn't left and *Dat's* expression was grim.

Charlie approached them first as they entered. "Why are those men here?"

"They have the mistaken impression that one of you is the daughter of a celebrity." Her father frowned. "I have no idea why."

"Will they leave?" Leah asked. She felt the constriction in her chest tighten.

"I hope so," *Mam* said. "What should we do?"

"Ignore them," *Dat* said. "Eventually they'll grow tired of waiting and go."

Ellie stared outside. "Doesn't look like they plan to leave anytime soon." She faced her parents. "What if they stay the night? I have to work tomorrow. How can I leave if they're still out there in the morning?"

"Let's not worry until it happens," her father said reasonably.

It was early in the day. How would they manage their daily lives if they couldn't go outside for fear that they would be accosted by an English news reporter with a camera and a microphone?

Leah put on a pot of coffee. "Anyone for a piece of pie?"

"I am," Charlie said, and the rest of the family echoed her response.

They sat, drank coffee and ate pie while they talked about what they'd do in the event the news van remained on the property.

"I can call the police on my cell phone," Ellie suggested.

"Not yet," *Dat* said. "Let's ignore them and maybe they will leave us in peace."

Her sisters helped Leah clean up while her parents stayed at the kitchen table. Ellie excused herself to go upstairs and call her client on today's schedule. Charlie decided to put in a load of laundry. Leah remained behind to dry the dishes and put them away while her parents grew silent at the table behind her.

When she was done, she hesitated. She wanted to

ask them if the reporters were here for her. She kept her mouth shut, unwilling to cause friction between her parents and her. She started to leave the room.

"Leah," her father said. "Would you come and sit? 'Tis time we told you what you've wanted to know."

Swallowing against a suddenly dry throat, Leah sat across from her parents.

"Leah," Missy began, "please know that we love you, and we want only the best for you."

"I love you," Leah said sincerely.

Her mother smiled, but her father's expression was unreadable.

"'Tis true that we adopted you when you were an infant," *Dat* said. "We thought it best to keep the truth from you because we wanted a normal life for you." He waited for Leah's nod before he continued. "You may not be our daughter by birth, but you are ours—never doubt that. You are a part of this family." He exchanged a brief, warm look with his wife. "Your mother was Missy's sister. She got pregnant during her senior year of high school. She couldn't take care of you, so she brought you to us—and we were thrilled."

"You're my aunt and uncle?" she whispered, floored by the knowledge.

"We were until we held you in our arms and took you for our own. From the first moment I laid eyes on you, I loved you," her father confessed huskily.

Tears filled Leah's eyes. Her father wasn't usually verbal with his affection, and she was deeply moved. "Who is my birth father?"

"He was Christine's high school sweetheart. He loved her. She never told him about you because Jason had big dreams. Chris loved him and didn't want to interfere with his plans. She never told him that she was carrying his child. If he'd known, he would have insisted on marrying her. She let him go, then after you were born, she brought you to us."

"May I see my birth mother? Meet her?"

Pain flickered across her mother's features. "'Tis not possible." She drew a sharp breath as if bracing herself for what she must reveal. "Your mother was killed in a car accident two months after you were born." Tears welled in her eyes. "Before she died, she frequently came to see you, but as your aunt not your mother. She wanted you to be happy, and we promised we'd take *gut* care of you." She sniffed. "We tried."

"You've always taken *gut* care of me," Leah said huskily. A tear escaped to trail down her cheek. "And my father?"

"He doesn't know about you," *Dat* said. "At least, we don't think he does, but now that those news people are outside, we've wondered..."

Leah frowned. "Why would those reporters care who my birth father is?"

"Your father's name is Jason Kingsley. He left home for a career in music. We don't know if he made it, so we can't be sure," her father explained. "Those men outside are looking for Derek Rhoades's daughter. The man is a musician, a singer and a rock star. We can't be certain, but it's possible that Derek Rhoades is the name Jason took for his music career."

Her pulse rate jacked up as Leah tried to process what her parents had told her. "He's not Amish?"

Mam shook her head. "I didn't grow up Amish, Leah. I chose to join the Amish church after I fell in love with your *vadder*." Her face was soft as she regarded her husband lovingly.

"So what will we do if they won't leave?" Leah asked as she glanced toward the window.

"We ignore them for as long as we can. You are our daughter—and no one else's. They have no proof that you are anyone else." To her surprise, her father reached across the table to clasp her hand. "I know you are mad at us, but I hope you still trust us."

"I trust you," she murmured. "And I'm not angry with you. I know you did what you thought was best, what my birth mother wanted you to do." She paused. "Was she kind? Your sister, Christine?"

Mam's expression filled with sadness. "She was a sweet girl who was desperately in love with her boyfriend. She sacrificed her happiness so that Jason could have the life he wanted. If that isn't kind…"

"'Tis more than kind," Leah whispered. She stood and peered out the window. "They're still there."

"They'll grow tired," *Dat* assured her.

"What if our faces make English TV news? What if Derek Rhoades believes the gossip and shows up?" she asked.

Her father stood. "Then we will deal with him when he does."

How? Leah wondered. *"Oll recht."* She hesitated, then asked, "What will you tell my sisters?"

"The truth," *Mam* said.

"Then they'll know I'm not their real sister."

"You are their sister, and they will be the first to say so."

Ellie and Charlie entered the room with identical confused expressions. "Why isn't Leah our sister?" Charlie asked *Mam*.

"Because I'm adopted," Leah said quietly.

"So?" Ellie's smile was warm as she gazed at Leah. "You *are* my sister."

"And *mine*," Charlie added.

Tears rushed to her eyes again. "But you don't know the circumstances…"

"We don't have to know. We love you," Ellie said.

Leah narrowed her gaze as she stared at her. "You overheard us."

Her sister shrugged. "Some of what you said but not all."

"Enough to know why that news van is camped outside our *haus*," her father said in a scolding tone.

Ellie shrugged. "Wouldn't matter if we hadn't eavesdropped, although that wasn't why we came back." She grinned. "We were hungry for sweets. We want coffee cake."

Missy laughed. "I should have known."

Her sisters joined them at the table, and the family decided to ignore the media and simply enjoy one another's company.

An hour later Leah peeked outside and cheered. "They're gone. The van and the reporters have left!"

"Thanks be to *God*," her father said, and they all echoed his prayer.

Two hours later, the newsmen returned, but there were three vehicles instead of one, and more men with cameras.

Leah saw them first. "*Dat!* The *Englishers* are back!"

Henry stood on the front porch of his sister and her husband's home and said his goodbyes. "You'll think about coming home for a visit?" he asked Ruth. "*Mam* and *Dat* miss you. We all do."

Ruth exchanged glances with her husband, John, who nodded. "I didn't know that *Dat* had a heart attack," she murmured with concern. She'd been upset to find out that Henry had written her and she'd never received his letter.

"He had two," Henry replied, "but he's doing well, especially since the doctor changed his medicine." He paused to study his sister. "They didn't want to worry you."

She sighed, because she understood her father. "But if he hadn't made it…"

"I'll make sure to call you if anything happens again."

She was only slightly mollified. "I'll call the store to let you know when we plan to come."

"Soon, I hope."

"Within the month," John said. "Hopefully within the next two weeks."

Henry smiled. "I enjoyed my visit. *Danki* for having me."

"As short as it was," Ruth complained.

"I need to get back." He'd decided that business was all he would do. Visiting Leah's grandparents would be the last thing she'd want, and he realized that he'd be breaking his promise about keeping her secret. He was ready to go home and see her. On the way here, he'd thought long and hard about what to do with Brad Smith. He decided that the next time he encountered the man, he would stand up to the *Englisher* no matter the consequences.

Henry looked down at the four boys who stood near their parents. "Bye, nephews. Be *gut* for your *mudder*."

"*Onkel* Henry, when can we see you again?" asked little Caleb, the youngest son at five years old.

"Soon," he promised with a grin for his sister, who tried to hide a smile.

Harley, who was a year older than Caleb, said, "When we come, can we see your store?"

Henry nodded. "You may, but the store isn't mine. It belongs to your *grossmammi* and *grossdaddi*."

"Where do you work then?" Caleb piped up.

"I help out in the store and—"

"Then the store is yours, too!" Harley insisted.

Henry laughed. "I guess so." He studied his sister's two older boys thoughtfully. "I like to build things. I can show you when you come," he told Aaron, aged eight, and John Junior, aged ten. "Would you like that?"

The boys bobbed their heads. With a sigh, he met his sister's gaze. "I have to go. I'll see you within the month." To his surprise, Ruth gave him a hug. Henry exchanged handshakes with his brother-in-law. "Take care. And *danki* for caring for my sister and nephews."

John's blue eyes twinkled. "They're not too much work."

Ruth gasped with outrage and tapped her husband on the arm, and Henry cracked up, with John quickly joining in the laughter.

Henry climbed into the hired car, waved and was soon on his way home. He missed the warmth of Leah's blue eyes and sweet smile. He hadn't been gone long so he doubted that she knew he'd gone away. Especially since it was Tuesday and the last time he'd spent time with her was Sunday.

It was a five-hour car's ride from Charm, Ohio, where his sister and her family lived, to his home in Happiness, Pennsylvania. It was early morning, and he should get back to his Amish community by two thirty in the afternoon at the latest. The first thing he'd do, once he dropped off his suitcase and spoke with his parents, would be to drive over to see Leah.

His heart beat rapidly at the thought. His stomach felt as if it was filled with fluttering butterflies. He was so eager to see Leah again that he'd head to wherever she'd gone if she wasn't at home.

Chapter Thirteen

"There have been news vans outside the Arlin Stoltzfus place since yesterday morning," Henry's mother said.

"News vans? Why?" Henry felt a lurch in his chest. He was worried about Leah. What had happened to bring the attention of English television?

"They claim one of the Stoltzfus girls is the daughter of someone famous. A singer-musician by the name of Derek Rhoades."

His heart raced, but he didn't let on that he had his suspicions, for it would mean giving away Leah's secrets. "Which daughter?"

Mam shook her head. "I don't know. It's not right. We all know that every one of those girls belong to Missy and Arlin. They all look like them."

Henry agreed. Leah had found proof of her adoption, but she did look like her adoptive parents, especially Missy. "Has anyone been able to get through to the *haus*?"

"*Nay*, the news people are like vultures, waiting to pounce on anyone who goes in or out. Noah Lapp drove by and was stopped by one. That's how he learned what was going on."

"This must be difficult for them," he said softly.

His mother regarded him with a knowing look. "You're worried about Leah."

He opened his mouth to deny it but found himself telling the truth. "*Ja.* I wish I could help her. Be there with her."

"You could try," she suggested. "Sneak in from the road at the back of the property."

Henry firmed his resolution. "I'll go now."

"Not until you've eaten," *Mam* insisted. "You've been traveling for hours. 'Tis late and you haven't had lunch."

"Mam."

"Henry." Her voice was firm and final. "I'd like to send supplies with you. I'm sure they have plenty of food, but it will make me feel better if you bring more. If you're staying there with her, you'll need to eat."

Within a half hour later, Henry drove his buggy to the Adam Troyer residence, which was located down the road from the Stoltzfus dwelling. He parked in the barnyard, then stopped for a brief word with Adam about leaving his vehicle before he headed on foot toward Leah's house. He cut through from the back of Arlin's property as his mother suggested. He kept hidden so that he could check out the situation without anyone catching sight of him. He made an effort to stay low as he ran from one bush or tree to another toward the house. He froze when he caught sight of several large news vehicles with round disks on their roofs parked in Arlin's driveway. The *Englishers* congregated in the yard. Some stood with large cameras ready to film anyone exiting the house. Others owned small handheld devices with the hope of taking photos of members of the Stoltzfus family. As he watched from behind a honeysuckle bush, he saw Arlin exit the house onto the porch.

"I told you that there is no one here of interest. I don't know where you got your information, but the girls inside the *haus* are my daughters. You are bothering my family and scaring my girls. You need to leave immediately. If you don't, we'll call the police."

"With what?" one man taunted. "You don't have a phone."

Henry's heart started to beat hard when Leah stepped out onto the porch to stand next to her father. She looked beautiful and upset…and very pale. He longed to go to her, call out to her, but remained still and silent. "We have a cell phone," she said loudly. "Our church elders have allowed it."

One man raised a camera to take a photo.

"Nay," she cried as she blocked her face with her hand to stop him from taking her picture. "'Tis forbidden to have our pictures taken. Go away!"

"Maybe we should leave," said a young man to the older one with the camera. "These people don't lie. They're telling the truth. We should leave them in peace."

The cameraman glared at him. "All people lie under the right circumstances."

"Leah, go inside," Arlin ordered.

Once Arlin and Leah had gone inside, Henry slipped away. To get caught outside their house would only draw more attention to the family. He would go home and return after dark. Surely, the news people would be long gone by then.

But first he would head to the store and, using their

new cell phone, call the police. Someone needed to order those awful reporters away. Maybe the police would order them gone, and the men would listen.

"*Dat*, what are we going to do?" Leah cried. "Maybe I should give them an interview."

"Nay," her father said. "You are my daughter. We don't even know who Derek Rhoades is. And they don't know that you are adopted. We need to keep the secret, or they will never leave us alone."

"But Derek Rhoades could be Jason Kingsley, *ja*?" she asked quietly as she fought back panic.

"'Tis possible, but not likely."

"If you go outside again, then I'll go with you. If you tell them you're adopted, then I will, too," Charlie said with a fierceness that startled Leah.

"Me, too," Ellie added with determination. "And I'll call Nell and Meg to say the same."

"Why would you do that?" Leah's eyes swam with tears. She wished Henry was here. He had the habit of making her feel good about herself.

"Because we are sisters…always have been and always will be."

She wiped her wet cheeks with the back of her hand. "But it will ruin your life."

"It will ruin yours if we don't stick together." Ellie moved to the window and stared outside. "I say we ignore them. If you go, then we will, too, but why should we give those awful people what they want?"

"Exactly," *Dat* said. "Stay inside. If they don't leave soon, Ellie, use your phone to call the police." Ellie nodded.

"I'm going upstairs to watch them from our bedroom window," Charlie declared. "Anyone want to come with me?"

"I will," Ellie said with a quick look in Leah's direction before they left.

Soon Leah and her parents were alone. "I'm sorry," Leah said. "I love you, and I'd give anything to stop this intrusion into our lives."

In a move that caused Leah a rush of emotion, her father encircled her with strong arms. He gave her a firm hug before releasing her. "I have loved you since the first time I saw you. I'd do anything for you as I would for any of my *dechter*. Don't worry. I'll take care of this."

"This isn't a thunderstorm, *Dat*," she whispered, referring to the time he'd rescued her when she was a young child.

"*Nay*, thunderstorms are more frightening," he answered and then grinned.

Leah chuckled through her tears. How could she not when her father was beaming at her. Concern made her look toward her mother. *"Mam."*

"I've known, Leah," her mother confessed. "About your fear of thunderstorms, but your *vadder* didn't tell me. I agree with him. This is easy compared to knowing your daughter is afraid and not being able to acknowledge it or do anything about it."

Leah gave her a sad half smile. "I'd like to be upstairs with Ellie and Charlie."

Her father nodded. "Don't worry, Leah. With God's help, we will get through this."

She hurried up the steps and entered Ellie's bedroom. "What are they doing?"

"Nothing," Ellie said with a grim face. "Absolutely nothing. They won't leave."

"Maybe this has gone on long enough," Charlie said. "You should call 911, Ellie."

Ellie picked her phone up from the windowsill and flipped it open. "*Ach nay*, I can't make the call," she cried. "The battery is dead!"

"Can't you charge it?" Charlie asked, clearly without a clue about the charging of cell phones.

"Where?" Ellie challenged. "I need electricity. I usually plug it in to charge wherever I'm working, but since I couldn't clean *haus* today..."

Leah gave her a reassuring smile. "'Tis fine, Ellie. We'll manage. I'm sure they'll leave us alone eventually."

Ellie looked dismayed as Charlie stared out the window. Her sisters wanted to go out, but they were forced to stay inside.

"I'm sorry," Leah told them.

"You have nothing to apologize for, Leah," her sisters uttered simultaneously.

As she stared into the yard, Leah's longing for Henry grew. Her sisters now knew about her adoption, but it was Henry she'd confided in...trusted. He had a way about him that soothed her and made her feel better.

She frowned. *Where is he? Surely, he's heard about the news crews staking out the* haus. Was he afraid to get involved? Had she been wrong about him? To believe that he cared enough to come when she needed him? Not that she had sent him a message, but she'd caught sight of her cousins Noah and Isaac, who'd driven by the property separately. Isaac would have hurried to tell Henry, wouldn't he?

Why isn't he here?

* * *

Henry waited until it was night before heading back to the Stoltzfus family. He'd explained his intent to Adam Troyer. He parked in the Troyer yard again and walked to Leah's. It was easier for him to approach the house in the dark. He caught sight of a light in the driveway to the house, but it was clear that all but one vehicle remained with a crew who were either too stubborn or they didn't care about consequences should the police return to discover them still on the premises.

He crept closer, keeping an eye on the crew and the front porch. Which door should he try? Would they answer and let him in? He moved carefully as he debated where to go when he heard someone call out.

"*Hey, you!* I want to talk with you! What do you know about the Stoltzfus sisters?"

Henry shot out into the night, eager to escape. He had the darkness and his knowledge of the property in his favor as he fled. It was only as he reached the road that he realized they could easily drive around and find him. He kept off the street, choosing instead to run across neighboring land until he reached the Troyers. He knocked on Adam's door.

"Please stay inside," he told the man. "The reporters saw me. I escaped, but they may knock on your door. It would be best if you don't open it."

Adam nodded. "What are you going to do?"

"I'll wait a few minutes, and if they don't come, I'll drive home. This has gone on long enough. Tomorrow I'm calling the police again. Those men need to leave the family alone."

"May the Lord be with you."

"*Danki* for your help, Adam."

The man smiled. "I will see you on Sunday if not before. Feel free to park here whenever you need to."

Henry nodded his thanks. "Do James and Nell know what's going on?" he asked, referring to Leah's sister and her husband, James, who was Adam's stepson.

"I don't know. Please call them. James has a phone."

Henry left a short while later, after he felt sure that no one had followed him. He decided to go to the store and call the police again. There was no sense waiting until the morning. The officer who took the call assured him that someone would be out to the property this evening.

After he hung up the phone, he realized that the only thing he could do at this moment was head up to the house.

The next morning, after a fitful night's sleep, Henry returned to the Arlin Stoltzfus property and was pleased to see that the reporters finally had left. With a sense of satisfaction, he approached the house but took the precaution of advancing from the back of the property. He knocked on the back door and Missy Stoltzfus answered it.

"Is Leah home?" Henry asked. "I was wondering if I could see her."

"I'm afraid she's sleeping. She's had a rough couple of days."

"Will you tell her that I stopped by?"

Missy smiled. "Of course."

"Danki." He returned her smile. "I'll stop by later if you think she'll be awake."

Missy retied her apron strings. "I can't promise but feel free."

Henry turned away. He halted and faced her again, but Leah's mother had already shut the door. He was eager to see Leah and disappointed that she wasn't available, but he understood. These last days must have been awful for her. There was so much he wanted to tell her. Like how much he loved her. He prayed that she returned his love.

He came back in the afternoon, but this time it was Arlin who answered the door. "*Hallo*, Arlin. Is Leah awake? I know she's had a difficult time."

Arlin stepped back and gestured for him to enter. While Leah's father's disappeared to find her, Henry enjoyed the warm coziness of their family kitchen. There was something delicious smelling baking in the oven. He was admiring his surroundings when Arlin returned. "I'm sorry, Henry, but Leah still isn't ready to see anyone."

Henry experienced a tightening in his chest. "Do you know when she'll be ready for visitors?"

The man shook his head. "I'll tell her to contact you when she is."

He left then, feeling as if she knew he was there and had decided to avoid him. Why? Had he done something wrong? He'd tried to help her by calling the police. He'd done the best he could under the circumstances. He'd tried to get through to her, but the reporters had made it impossible to get to the house without being accosted by them.

Henry decided he would return again and again until Leah agreed to talk with him. If she didn't want to see him again, she'd have to tell him to his face. The notion made his stomach burn.

He climbed into his buggy and drove home. He'd driven only a mile or so when a car pulled up alongside him. He ignored it and kept driving, shaken to see Brad Smith, who laughed and waved at him before he sped off.

The next morning, he went to the Stoltzfus residence. When her sister Ellie tried to put him off, Henry couldn't stop himself from pushing inside.

"Please," he begged. "I need to see her. I have to see Leah."

Ellie stared at him a long moment and something softened in her expression. "I'll get her," she said quietly.

Leah mended clothes as she sat by the window in her room. She'd witnessed Henry's arrival and told Ellie that she didn't want to see him. He looked so handsome that he stole her breath. He wore no hat, and his dark hair was tousled as if he'd run his fingers through it. The depth of her feelings for him scared her. *He didn't come when I needed him.* How could she rely on a man who stayed away because it was inconvenient for him to deal with the reporters?

She set aside the mended shirt and dropped her head into her hands. She loved Henry, and she shouldn't. She needed to keep distance between them so that she could get over her love for him.

Ellie appeared in her doorway. "Henry refuses leave. He says he needs to talk with you."

"Ellie."

"I think you should see him, Leah. Find out what he has to say." Her sister stared. "He seems desperate to see you."

"I thought he would come when the reporters were here," she confessed softly. "I needed him and I thought he would come but he didn't."

"Maybe he didn't know what was happening," her sister reasoned.

"How could he not? Everyone else in our community knew. Word spreads quickly throughout our community. And the media was here long enough."

"You need to come down. If you have something to say to him, then say it. If you don't want to see him again, you need to tell him face-to-face."

Leah stood. "Fine." She brushed down the folds of her pale blue dress, checked to make sure her prayer *kapp* was on straight, then went downstairs to see the one person she feared seeing the most because of her overwhelming love for him. Henry Yoder was the only man who had ever made her feel feminine and vulnerable…and alive.

She entered the kitchen to find him standing near the back door with his hat in his hands.

"Leah." Henry gazed at her with longing in his blue eyes, and Leah felt her heart skip a beat before it settled into a rapid, steady rhythm. "Are you *oll recht*?"

His look of tenderness nearly undid her. She fought against the weakness and pretended to be strong. "I'm fine, Henry. I'm surprised to see you here. Why have you come?"

"I wanted—needed—to see you, Leah." A small smile curved his lips. "I've missed you."

She looked away, unwilling to fall for this. He was the only person who had the power to hurt her. "I thought you'd come sooner."

"I tried," he admitted. "I couldn't get near the *haus*."

"You mean you didn't try hard enough."

He slowly approached. "Leah, I did try."

She narrowed her gaze. "I don't believe you." She'd needed him and he hadn't been there for her. "I think you should leave."

Henry shook his head. "Please, Leah. I'd like to explain. *Please.* I was out of town for a night. I didn't know what happened until I returned. I tried to get to you immediately..."

Skeptical, Leah folded her arms across her chest and stared. "You need to go, Henry. I don't want to talk now. I'm tired and I need peace. I'm not up for a discussion with you." When he slumped as if in defeat, she firmed her resolve to prevent herself from running to him and begging him to love her as much as she loved him.

"May I come by tomorrow? Can we talk then?" he asked quietly.

She shook her head. "I don't think that's wise."

"Why not?"

"We worked together such a short time, Henry. Why would you think that I'd want or need to see you again?" Her chest tightened as she uttered the falsehood. She prayed for God's forgiveness.

A flash of pain darkened his blue eyes, then was gone so quickly that she thought she'd imagined the change. "I won't bother you again, Leah." He turned and opened the door. "I care for you, Leah," he said without facing her. "A great deal. I...I thought we'd become friends, and I'd hoped for more." He was silent for several seconds but didn't turn. Yet, he still didn't leave. "Take care of yourself." His voice was husky and thick with emotion.

Then Henry Yoder walked out of the house and possibly out of her life, and Leah knew that she'd never be the same again.

Chapter Fourteen

He'd wanted to be there for her. Hadn't he tried to get to her? And he'd done what he could to help. He'd called the police twice. As he left the Stoltzfus property, Henry felt terrible. Leah was mad at him and told him she never wanted to see him again. He grew thoughtful as he steered his buggy home. *Why is she so angry?*

As he entered the house minutes later, Henry saw his mother.

"You went to see Leah?" she asked knowingly.

"Ja."

"How did it go?"

Henry shook his head. "Not well. She's upset with me. She asked me to leave."

"Why?"

"Something about not being there for her," he mumbled.

"You tried to see her. Called the police to help."

"I know, but she didn't want to listen." He paused. "I don't know what to do."

"You love her," his *mam* said softly.

He met her glance, then looked away. "*Ja*, I do."

"Then you need to keep trying. She's had a rough time. Maybe she just needs to rest."

Henry met his mother's gaze with a feeling of hope. "Do you think so?"

Mam inclined her head. "I've seen the way she looks at you."

"How?"

"Like she cares for you. She may be scared, Henry. Leah has never had a sweetheart. And I suspect she feels the same way that you do, but she's afraid to trust her feelings for you."

He froze with disbelief. Could it be true? Did she care for him but was afraid to give in to her feelings? Was she so frightened of getting hurt that she'd chosen to withdraw from him?

He smiled. He'd never hurt Leah. In fact, the only thing he wanted to do was love and care for her…and protect her. No matter what she'd said, he wouldn't—couldn't—stay away from her, not if there was a chance that he might have her in his life forever. *As my wife.*

Henry sighed. He would see Leah again and he would convince her that they were meant to be together. They had become friends during their working relationship and his feelings for her had grown. *I love her.* Now he had to get her to admit that their love should be given a chance. He'd give her until this afternoon before approaching her again. He said so to his mother.

"Do you think that's wise?" she asked with concern.

"I have to see her, *Mam.* I don't think I can wait until tomorrow."

She looked as if she understood. "I have to visit Katie Lapp at three. I'll drop you off on my way, then pick you up on my way home."

“I can walk,” he said with a smile. ““It isn’t too terribly far, and if she rejects me again, I’ll need the exercise to think about what to do next.”

What have I done? Leah sat up in bed, horrified that she’d sent Henry away. She’d been tired and frustrated—and angry with what had happened. How had the reporters found out that one of them was adopted? Who had dug deep enough to bring more than four news companies to the front of their house?

She wanted to see Henry and apologize. She rose from bed and got ready to leave for Yoder’s Store. She recalled the quick flash of hurt she’d seen in his eyes and felt her chest constrict with pain.

She checked to make sure that her hair was neatly pinned and tucked up under her prayer *kapp.* She wore her light blue dress and looked to make sure it wasn’t soiled or wrinkled. Satisfied with her appearance, she headed downstairs, wondering why she cared how she looked. She’d never given in to vanity before, and it bothered her that she had now. *I want to look nice for Henry.* Would he forgive her?

Leah entered the kitchen and froze at the sight of strange men seated with her mother and father at the kitchen table. When her parents saw her, their expressions filled with concern. As she turned to study the two men, she found her gaze held by the man who was so handsome that she was taken aback.

“I’m sorry, I didn’t mean to disturb you,” she said as she turned away.

“Sit down, Leah,” her *dat* said quietly. She obeyed, choosing to sit next to her mother. “Leah, this is Derek Rhoades and his manager, John Markinson.”

"Hello, Leah," Derek said. It was his looks that first caught her attention.

"Why are you here?" she asked, suddenly feeling shaky.

"To apologize for all the problems you'd had with the press."

"I see."

"And to meet my daughter for the first time."

She blinked with shock. "Your daughter?" she replied huskily. She looked to her mother for confirmation.

Mam dipped her head. "Derek's real name is Jason Kingsley."

Leah stared at her biological father. Her heart beat hard as she tried to study him objectively. "Why now?"

Derek seemed taken aback by the question, then he laughed. "You are just like your mother," he murmured, clearly pleased.

"My mother is sitting beside me." She exchanged glances with Missy, whose eyes had filled with tears.

"I know." Derek's voice became soft. He gave her a sad smile before he turned to Missy. "You've done an amazing job with her."

"We love her," her *dat* said, and Leah reached under the table to squeeze his hand. He seemed shocked, but then he met her gaze with his love for her shining in his brown eyes.

"I'm not here to interfere," her biological father said. "I just found out about you a week ago. As much as I wanted to meet you, I was going to stay away." He frowned. "I don't know how the information leaked to the press, but I'm sorry it did. It wasn't my intention to hurt you and...your family."

Leah eyed him closely, noting the tired lines about his eyes, the dark shadows that told her that he hadn't slept in several days. "Did you love my birth mother?"

He rubbed the back of his neck. "Yes, I did, and I was foolish enough to believe that my music career should come first, so I left." Pain flashed in his blue eyes. "Chris encouraged me to go. She said she was proud of me for chasing my dream." He released a shaky breath. "We kept in touch during those first months I was gone. Then suddenly I didn't hear from her, and I admit I was so caught up in the growing success of my band and career that time seemed to get away from me. The next time I tried to call her, I learned that her phone had been disconnected. I wrote but never heard, so I figured she'd moved on with someone else."

Listening quietly, Leah felt an odd mixture of sympathy and dismay for a young couple who had loved and lost. "She never told you about me."

Derek shook his head. "No. I learned what happened to Christine only recently after I hired a private investigator to find her. That's when I learned about the car accident—" he blinked rapidly, clearly overcome with emotion "—and that she'd had a child eight months after I'd left. I knew her child was mine. Chris and I were exclusive." When Leah arched an eyebrow in question, he tried to smile before he said, "We were in love and saw only each other."

She nodded. She waited a moment, then asked, "What do you want from me?"

The man opened his mouth to answer, but his manager beside him replied for him. "He came to apologize about the barrage of media. He wants you to live happily and in peace."

Leah felt a rush of emotion as she thought of Henry Yoder. She could be happy with Henry and she always felt peaceful in his company. "Thank you," she said sincerely.

Derek beamed at her. "I've given your parents my private cell phone number. Should you ever have trouble again, please let me know. I'll put a stop to it."

"You can do that?"

"Yes." His tone was clipped, determined.

She studied him with fresh eyes and saw what her birth mother, Christine, had seen in him. And it wasn't just because of his looks. If this man had chosen a different path, then she would have had a different life with a different father and mother. She glanced at her *mam* and *dat*, and was glad that her life had ended up this way. "I'm sorry for your loss," she said, referring to Christine. Her birth mother, Missy's sister, might have died right after she was born, but he'd just learned of her death and his loss was still new and raw.

Her birth father appeared surprised, but then he understood. "Thank you," he whispered. He took one last sip from the coffee that her mother had fixed for him, then stood. "We should go."

Leah rose, as did her parents. "It was nice to meet you. To know the truth," she said as she accompanied him toward the door.

He stopped and faced her. "Leah, should you or your family ever need anything—anything at all—please call me. I'll always be happy to help my daughter and her loving family."

"Thank you," she said politely, trying not to feel more for this man who was her birth father. Now that she'd met him and understood the circumstances surrounding her adoption, she felt satisfied and more eager to see Henry.

Derek raised his hand as if to touch her cheek but then promptly dropped it, as if realizing how wrong the action would be, especially to a woman who had been raised and still was a member of an Amish community. He shifted his gaze to Missy. "Thank you." He turned to Arlin and held out his hand. "Thank you for loving her." He spun back to open the door and stepped outside. Leah heard him curse beneath his breath.

"Stay inside," he ordered.

It was a lovely day as Henry started the two-mile walk that would bring him to Leah. The sun was warm, but a summer breeze kept it from being too hot or humid. He stayed just off the shoulder of the road. He knew that cars often sped by and he didn't want to take any chances. With Leah in his life, he had too much to live for. He passed a yard where the scent of honeysuckle reached out to tease his nose. He smiled and picked up his pace. He wanted—needed—to see Leah, and now he wished he'd waited for his mother to drive him so he could get to her faster.

He heard a car come up from behind him but paid it no mind and moved farther off the road. It was only when the driver pulled his car to block Henry's path that he looked up, startled. He groaned as he watched Brad Smith get out of his vehicle. The last person he needed to see right now was the *Englisher*. He'd already made up his mind to stand up to Brad, and he would.

"Henry," Brad said in a taunting voice. "Enjoying your walk?"

He shrugged. "It's a nice day for one." He gazed at the man and sighed. "What do you want, Brad?"

"A little payback."

Henry frowned. "For what?"

"For my years spent in prison."

"I didn't put you there. You went a long time after that night at Whittier's Store." He stared. "Might have something to do with your sister?"

Brad bristled. "What do you know about my sister? Do you know where she is?"

"No." He didn't move, although he longed to push past the man so that he could get to Leah.

"I don't believe it. Tell me where she is."

"I told you I don't know where she is."

"Then you'll pay."

The hit came out of nowhere. Pain lanced Henry's check as he fell to the ground. He scrambled to his feet and was promptly slugged again. He didn't fight. It was against the *Ordnung*, so he took the man's punches to his head, his shoulder, his stomach, and he fell to his knees, gasping for breath.

"Stop!" a familiar male voice demanded. Henry could barely make out his friend Jeff Martin's image as it wavered before him. The Englisher and his father often gave rides to members of his community. "Get away from him!"

Brad stepped back, held up his hands. "I don't want no trouble," he complained.

"Yet you're beating on a man who won't fight back," Jeff said. "Henry's faith won't allow him to hit you back, you coward!"

Henry felt a gentle hand help him to his feet.

"Are you all right?" Jeff asked softly.

"I'm fine." But he felt woozy and he teetered on his feet as he stood.

Immediately Jeff slipped his arm around Henry's waist to support him. "I'm taking you to the hospital."

"*Nay!* I need to go to Leah's. I need to see her."

"But you're hurt badly. You can see her after you've received medical attention."

But Henry continued to shake his head. Every movement intensified his pain, but he didn't care. No one would keep him from seeing Leah Stoltzfus. "I'll go after I see her. I need to see her. *Please.*"

"Leah Stoltzfus?"

"Yes," Henry whispered.

"I'll drive you." Jeff said "But then I'll be driving you to the hospital with no arguments."

Henry managed to smile although he had a cut lip, and all of his injuries throbbed terribly. "Thank you."

"Don't thank me. I'm not doing you a favor by waiting."

A police siren heralded the arrival of the authorities, who caught Brad as he tried to leave, but his car wouldn't start.

"Finally," Jeff said with satisfaction. Henry heard Brad's loud complaints interspersed with whining as he was pulled from his vehicle and shoved into the back of the police car. "Thank you, Officer," he called loudly.

"He won't bother anyone again," the uniformed policeman said. "The fellow has an outstanding arrest warrant."

Henry sighed with relief. "I hope he is put away longer than the last time."

A second officer stood back from Brad's vehicle and held up a clear bag filled with a white substance. "There will be extra charges filed against him. He won't walk anytime soon."

The officers left as Jeff gently helped Henry into the front seat of his SUV. "I still think you should go right to the hospital."

"No. Need to see Leah," he said. His pain was intense, but he fought back the darkness. He needed Leah. Had to make her understand. "Leah," he murmured as Jeff drove fast toward the Stoltzfus residence.

Chapter Fifteen

Leah heard Derek's sharp command, and after he and his manager stepped outside, she opened the door to see what was happening. She gasped. News vans filled with reporters were back, camped out on the edge of their property, apparently having learned of the celebrity's visit.

"Derek!" one man cried. "Come to see your daughter?"

"I came to apologize to this good family for your interference. If you think it's anything else, then you're mistaken."

"So you don't have a daughter who lives here?" another reporter called out. There was a cameraman beside him filming the encounter.

"The daughters in the house are Arlin and Missy Stoltzfus's," Derek replied politely. "So I'd thank you to stop filming on this property. Amish aren't allowed to have their photos taken. It's against their religion and a breach of their way of life." When the cameraman kept filming, he turned on the charm. "Please," he asked nicely.

The man lowered the camera and Derek flashed him a smile. "What are you doing in town then?" the reporter asked.

"I'm on tour. I was in the area and I'd heard what happened so I came."

"That's it?" a woman said with a snarky tone of disbelief.

Derek ramped up his famous charm. "Maybe. Maybe not. But it's not in this house." He hinted that there was another more personal reason for him to be in Lancaster County.

Sensing a diffusing of interest in her family, Leah stepped out onto the porch. Her parents and sisters quickly followed suit. She gazed at the news crews and her breath constricted. She wanted them to leave. She wanted to find Henry.

Derek and his manager were talking with the media. Derek was telling them about the fine women who lived in this part of Pennsylvania, and Leah saw how enthralled the media was with him. He was something to behold, Leah realized. All charm, dark good looks and charisma.

A car honked as it pulled onto the lawn to get past the news vehicles. Leah looked at the car with recognition. It was Jeff Martin. The man and his father often gave rides to the members of her community. She wondered what he was doing there and why the fanfare until her heart gave a lurch as she spied the man in the front passenger seat. Henry Yoder. She stared, fascinated, until Jeff got out and hurried to the other side of the car. Frowning, Leah watched as he reached in to assist Henry out of the vehicle. Leah took one look at the man she loved and gasped. He was injured. She got a quick glimpse of his bloody face and he could barely stand. She glanced at Derek, who was still close enough to hear her gasp. He encouraged her with his gaze, then he quickly led the media away from her, grabbing the media's focus as he headed toward the news vans.

Henry had his head bent with his hat pulled low to hide his face as he approached. She shot a look toward Derek and his manager, who were surrounded by the media. She faced Henry with concern. He was struggling as he tried to get to her. With a whimper of remorse, Leah ran to him.

She halted within a few feet of him and examined him thoroughly, noting the injuries to his poor face and neck, and the bruises on his lower arms. Where else was he injured? "What happened?" she asked softly with concern.

After hearing her voice, Henry raised his head until their gazes locked. "I have to talk with you."

She inhaled sharply. There was more blood on his face than she'd realized. A laceration across his left cheek. There was a darkening bruise around his right eye.

"I have to talk with you, too," she replied with the tears in her eyes. "Henry," she whispered. "You're hurt."

"I'll live."

"Not if I don't get you to the hospital soon," Jeff said darkly.

Leah eyed Jeff. "Why is Henry here then?"

"He wouldn't go," Jeff explained quietly, "until he had a chance to see you."

Her attention shifted to the man she loved. "Henry, about this morning..."

"Leah," he murmured as he swayed on his feet. "I love you. I know you don't want to see me, but I want a chance to change your mind. I need you in my life..."

"Henry," she admitted, "I love you, too." But he hadn't heard her, for he'd slumped to the ground, unconscious. *"Henry,"* she cried. "Jeff!"

"Get in the car," Jeff told her gently as he examined Henry with a concerned look. "I'm taking him to the hospital, and he'll want you to be there."

She nodded, then ran to her parents. "*Mam. Dat.* Henry..." She choked up, unable to continue.

"Go," her father said as if he correctly understood the situation. "We'll come when we can."

Jeff had put Henry onto the back seat, and Leah climbed in next to him. The *Englisher* had taken off Henry's hat, and Leah had the strongest urge to stroke Henry's soft dark hair, but she was afraid she'd hurt him. She picked up his hand, which seemed to be one of the few spots that were injury-free. *Because he didn't fight back.* She wove her fingers through his and stroked his hand with her thumb.

As his car sped toward the hospital, Jeff told her what had happened, ending with Brad being hauled away by police and Henry's insistence that he had to see her. Emotionally spent, Leah closed her eyes as she prayed hard and silently that Henry would recover fully.

He loves me. She continued to pray. *Please take care of him, Lord.* He'd insisted on seeing her before seeking medical attention. The idea was foolish and humbling. She realized just how much he cared for her, and she never stopped praying so that she could tell Henry as well as show him again and again just how much he meant to her.

* * *

Henry came to with a groan. He hurt all over. He didn't know where he was, but then the *beep, beep, beep* of a heart monitor made him realize he was in the hospital. And then it all came back to him. His encounter with Brad Smith, Jeff's arrival at a time when Henry had begun to wonder if the man would kill him before he was through. His hazy visit with Leah.

"Leah," he murmured.

"I'm right here," she assured him. "I'm not going anywhere."

He felt a light touch on his right hand and he opened his eyes. The sight of her beautiful face brought him to tears. "Leah, you're here," he whispered. The knowledge that she was close made him happy. He felt himself relax, then promptly fell asleep again.

When he awoke next, he was more alert. He glanced toward his right and saw Leah seated in a chair close to his bed. She was slumped against his mattress, her hand still holding his.

"You're awake," his mother said in a soft voice. "How are you feeling?"

"Sore."

She inclined her head. "I'll get the nurse. Maybe she can give you something for the pain."

He shook his head and winced at the painful movement. "Not yet. I don't want to sleep again." He glanced down with love at the woman who slept at his side. When he lifted his gaze again, it was to see his mother's warm expression and the knowledge that she was pleased and approved of the woman he loved. "How long has she been here?"

"All night. Since you were brought in yesterday afternoon."

Henry frowned. "She must be exhausted."

His mother smiled. "She wouldn't leave your side." She moved closer so that she could talk more quietly without waking up Leah. "She loves you. She's *gut* for you."

He gazed at his *mam* with the truth of his heart in his eyes. "Where's *Dat*?" he asked, needing to change the subject before he bawled like a baby.

"He went downstairs for coffee." She moved up toward his head. "Are you hungry?"

"Nay," he said softly. Leah murmured in her sleep, then shifted before she came abruptly awake. "Henry," she whispered, then she sat back and looked up at him, startled yet pleased to see him awake. "Henry, I've been so worried about you."

"So much that you were able to sleep." He gave her a teasing half grin, then gasped at the searing pain in his cheek.

"I haven't slept the whole time!" she insisted but then saw from his mother's expression what Henry had tried to do. To put aside her fear and concern for him by showing that he could joke with her as he fought pain. "Oh, you!"

"Henry," Arlin greeted as he and Missy entered his hospital room. "You're awake. That's *gut*." His voice was gruff, filled with concern.

Henry looked from one to the other before returning his attention to the woman he loved. "They were here yesterday and came back today," Leah said.

"We're glad you're on the mend," Missy said.

"Me, too." He switched positions of his and Leah's fingers so that it was he who caressed the back of her hand.

"Henry." Another man stepped forward. Henry had never met him before, so he eyed him with confusion. "Do you need anything?" the man said. "If you need anything at all, ask."

Henry glanced from the handsome *Englisher* who looked somehow similar to Leah, the woman he loved. His eyes widened. "Leah."

"Henry, this is Derek Rhoades, my birth father. Derek, meet Henry Yoder, the man I hope to marry someday."

Marry someday. Leah's words formed in his brain, and it was all Henry could process. He gazed at her, then at the man, and he drew a sharp breath. Pain shot through his ribs, overwhelming him, and his vision blurred.

"Henry." He heard Leah's voice from a distance. *"Henry!"*

And then Henry heard no more as his world receded, then went dark.

He woke again to the sound of a distressed feminine voice followed by assurances in deep male tones. He opened his eyes to see Leah talking anxiously with a tall *Englisher* while another one, a man who looked familiar, spoke with his and Leah's parents.

"Leah," he called out to her, his voice weak to his ears.

She spun and rushed to his side. "Henry, are you *oll recht*? You passed out and scared me."

"I'm sorry," he apologized.

The tall English man, who wore a doctor's white lab coat approached the bed. "Pain got too much for you," he said with a look of compassion. "You've two broken ribs. The pain can be unbearable enough to make you pass out. And we've been concerned because of your concussion." He bent close to examine him, telling him to look one way, then another, as he shone a light into his eyes. He studied the cut on Henry's cheek before he stepped back. "You'll live. Although I don't expect it wise to run up against another fist anytime soon," he joked.

Henry controlled his smile into a small crooked tilt of his lips. "Thank you, Doc."

The man faced the others. "I'm going to discharge him tomorrow morning. I think he'll feel much better recuperating at home."

The other *Englisher* stepped forward. "Is there anything he'll he need once he's home?"

"Her." The doctor smiled as he pointed toward Leah, who gazed raptly at Henry while she shifted closely toward the bed.

The dark-haired *Englisher* smirked. "Not mine to give, but you can ask her father," he said, shifting his gaze toward Arlin.

"We'll take care of him," Arlin said with determination and a warm look toward Henry, who felt his spirits rise.

The tall handsome man nodded, then approached the side of the bed where Leah stood. "At first, I thought Leah's introduction to me caused you to pass out." He gave him a crooked smile. "Until Dr. Morgan explained everything to us." He smiled at Henry. "I'm Derek Rhoades, also known as Jason Kingsley. Leah's birth father."

Henry's gaze flew to Leah, whose gaze remained locked on him. "You discovered the truth."

She nodded. "*Ja.* I know everything."

Henry studied her face and realized that she was fine with what she'd learned. He waved her closer until she'd bent close with her ear turned to hear his quiet words, meant only for her. "I love you, Leah Stoltzfus."

She pulled back and beamed at him.

"And that would be my cue to leave," Derek said with a chuckle. The man addressed everyone in the room, including Leah, before returning to Henry's side. "You're a lucky man, Henry."

"I know."

The man's expression turned serious. "Take care of her."

"I will. I promise."

Then Derek left, and their parents followed him, leaving Leah alone with Henry.

"Don't you want to see Derek off?"

She shook her head. "I'd rather be with you," she murmured, and to his surprise, she reached across his pillow to tenderly run her fingers through his hair.

He lifted a hand to caress her raised arm. "You need to go home and rest."

She scowled at him. "I don't want to leave."

"I'm not going anywhere until tomorrow morning. I'm going to need you rested and refreshed then."

"Are you saying that I look bad?"

"*Nay*, never that. You'll always look beautiful to me."

She sighed heavily, but there was a glimmer of happiness in her pretty blue eyes. "I'll go, but I'll be back first thing."

"Fine." He lowered his hand and closed his eyes,

as their conversation had tired him. She stood close and continued to run her fingers through his hair. He breathed a happy a sigh. “Go home, Leah. I love you.”

“I love you, too,” she whispered. Then he heard her leave, and he pressed the nurse call button. He was ready for his medicine that would help him sleep. He needed to heal quickly. There was so much he wanted to do with Leah. So much he wanted to say. And there were plans to be made.

“See you tomorrow, *soohn*,” his father said quietly a few minutes later. Henry opened his eyes, managed a tiny smile and nod. Then he fell asleep and dreamed pleasantly of Leah and the house they would live in and the babies they would have together.

Chapter Sixteen

Henry sat on the front porch of his family home and stared at the yard. He was on the mend, but his parents insisted he continue to rest and recuperate. He was feeling edgy. He hadn't seen Leah in several days, and he wanted nothing more than to go to her. But wouldn't she visit him if she loved him, as she'd claimed? Had something changed in their relationship? Something he wasn't aware of?

According to his mother, his black eye had faded to a soft yellow. He'd gone back to the doctor yesterday and learned that his cheek was healing nicely. The man had inspected his stitches and he was pleased with the look of the wound.

Where was Leah? Why wasn't she here? Henry scowled as he rose from his chair. If he could just get to his buggy before his parents saw him. It wasn't a long drive to the Stoltzfus residence. He'd be fine.

Movement in the yard heralded the return of his mother. Henry quickly plopped back into the chair, unwilling to openly disobey her order to rest and stay put, but he needed to go.

He waited for her to climb the porch steps before he spoke.

"I don't know why I have to sit here all day. I need to go out for a while." He needed to see Leah, to ensure that she really loved him the way he loved her.

"Your ribs aren't fully healed," Mam pointed out sternly.

"The doctor taped them up after x-raying them again yesterday. I can get around just fine. Please," he pleaded. "Let me take the buggy."

"Leah still hasn't been by to visit?"

He felt glum as he shook his head. "That's why I have to go. I have to make sure that nothing's changed between us."

"Henry."

"*Mam*, please. I haven't been anywhere. I haven't been to church services, and you wouldn't let me go to the Lapps' for Visiting Sunday."

His mother studied him thoughtfully. "She'll come to you when she's ready."

"I don't understand," he said. "Ready for what?" He experienced a clenching in his belly, a pain more powerful than his broken rib or cut cheek. "She's changed her mind and she is trying to find a nice way to let me down."

Mam shrugged. "You'll know soon enough," she said cryptically.

He must have looked devastated, because she approached him and placed a hand on his shoulder. "Trust in the Lord," she said. "If you and she are meant to be, you will be."

He glanced away as he fisted his hands in his lap. "I have to do something. Sitting here by myself is slowly killing me." He rose and, taller than her, he looked down to capture her gaze. "I'm going to the barn."

"The horses have been fed and watered."

"I'm not going for the horses," he said as he continued on his way. He felt fine, he assured himself. The slight twinge in his midsection was merely an inconvenience, nothing more.

"Henry."

"I'm sorry, *Mam*, but I have to do something." It might as well be something to keep his hands and, hopefully, his mind busy.

She kept silent then, but he could sense her disapproving gaze as he crossed the yard and entered the section of the barn where he built cabinets. He saw a project he'd started before he'd gotten injured. The freestanding combination cabinet and chest of drawers had been ordered for Barbara Martin, Rick Martin's wife and Jeff's mother. Rick had commissioned the work as a surprise for their wedding anniversary. He thought a moment, trying to recall the deadline Rick had given him. Neither Rick nor Jeff had stopped by to see the progress of the project, but Henry figured it was because both men were aware of his injuries and didn't want to rush him.

He picked up a drawer he'd made, eyed the size and shape of it, and knew he still had three more to make to finish the lower chest portion of the cabinet. He eyed the wood he'd selected for the work, picked up a medium-sized length, then promptly put it down as he realized that his parents were right. He wasn't up to doing anything but sitting inside or on the front porch. He wouldn't mind it if he had someone to keep him company. Actually, only one specific person to keep him company. *Leah Stoltzfus.*

Henry walked out of the barn and headed back to his chair on the porch. The sight of Leah Stoltzfus in the yard talking with his mother gave him pause.

"Henry," his mother said. The young woman turned around, and Henry was more than a little disappointed. It wasn't Leah in the yard; it was her sister Ellie, the other blonde Stoltzfus sister.

His steps slowed as he made his way back to the porch. To his surprise, Ellie followed him and waited until he was seated before moving to stand before him. Henry looked up into her eyes and then promptly shut them. He didn't want Ellie's visit. He wanted Leah.

"Henry," the young woman said. "Leah wanted me to give you this."

His eyes opened and he tried to read her expression before he glanced down at what she held. "She's been… ah…busy lately, and she wanted you to know that she was thinking about you."

She thrust a ceramic plate at him, then turned to leave. "She'll be by as soon as she can."

He couldn't answer her. His attention was caught at the chocolate-chip cookie on the plate. It was shaped in a heart and painted with icing. He read the words *Leah loves Henry* and felt the flutter in the region of his heart. A big smile stretched across his face.

"Ellie," he called to Leah's sister. She stopped as she was about to climb into her buggy. "Tell her I feel the same way about her."

Ellie's grin was sweet. "You'll have to tell you yourself the next time you see her."

"And when will that be?"

She shrugged. "I don't know."

Henry sighed. "I'll wait for her."

Ellie boosted herself into the buggy's driver seat. "That, I'll tell her." And then she left, leaving Henry with a renewal of hope and the anticipation of seeing Leah again.

An hour after Ellie's departure, another buggy approached down the drive and pulled close to the house. Henry, still seated on the front porch, stared at the buggy as Leah climbed out and approached. She carried a bag and a large dish.

He gazed at her. "What have you got there?"

She froze, as if something in his tone had upset her. "I brought you lunch."

"Why?"

"Because you have to eat." She appeared hesitant.

"*Mam* has food in the house."

"I thought you'd like to sit and eat with me."

"I'm already sitting."

Leah nodded. She was even more beautiful than he'd remembered. He wanted her with him until his last breath. "If I'm bothering you, I can go," she whispered, looking hurt.

"Don't you dare," he said huskily. "I need you to come here and sit by me as much as I need air." He regarded her with warmth, and her face cleared of worry, making her appear even more radiant. She sat next to him in silence, opened the bag on her lap and pulled out two more chocolate-chip cookies with icing messages.

He gazed into her eyes, then at her mouth, before studying what she held. He read *I miss you* on one cookie and *You're the only one for me* on the other. She looked embarrassed as she then pulled out two sandwiches made with fresh turkey. Henry studied the cookies, then the sandwich she gave him. "I only need those," he said, focusing his eyes briefly on the cookies before lifting to caress her with his gaze.

She didn't look away. "I'm sorry I haven't been by."

He swallowed hard. "Why haven't you?"

"I needed to find a place for my craft shop."

Hurt, he stared at her. "You didn't wait for me."

She shook her head.

"Why not?"

"You were recovering." She glanced at him shyly. "I know you told me you love me, but you were hurt and ill…and I wasn't sure."

"Yet, you made me cookies," he said.

He saw her hand tremble as she tucked back a lock of her hair. "I'm sorry. I don't know much about having a beau since I've never had one."

"And you never will," Henry said fiercely, which made Leah jerk with shock.

She stared at him with a tormented expression. "I see."

"*Nay*, you don't, Leah, because you don't need a beau. I have more in mind for you." He smiled when she blushed. He reached to grasp her hand. "I want to wed you, Leah Stoltzfus." He rose and with a grimace dropped down to one knee. "Leah, will you marry me? Be my love and my safe haven. Will you let me care for you, protect you and keep you forever?"

He heard her sob and saw tears fill her eyes. He stiffened with the belief that his proposal was unwelcome. "*Ja*, Henry Yoder," she breathed. "I'd love nothing more than to be your wife."

Still holding on to her hand, Henry climbed awkwardly to his feet, ignoring the twinge of pain left from his injured ribs. *"Praise the Lord!"* he shouted, overjoyed. He glanced over to see that her father had joined her mother in the yard, and both of them looked pleased as they gazed at the two of them.

Henry grabbed Leah's other hand so that he held each of her hands in one of his. "I love you desperately." He watched her features soften with love and her blue eyes shine with happy tears.

She sniffed. "I love you more."

He chuckled as he gazed at her with emotion. "Never, Leah. I'll always love you more." He inhaled sharply, then released the breath. *"Much more."*

Epilogue

Leah stood in her wedding dress in a room filled with women. Her dress was an azure blue, made for her by her mother. Three of her Lapp cousins' wives studied her with pleased expressions.

"It looks lovely," Rachel, her cousin Noah's wife, said. "The color's wonderful on you, Leah."

The other Lapp women agreed. Sarah and Annie beamed at her while her mother adjusted the white cape and apron and Ellie walked around to study Leah from every angle.

"Are you ready?" Ellie said.

"*Ja*, more than ever." Leah grinned. "I love him and can't wait to be his wife."

"On that note, I think 'tis time for us to leave," Sarah said with a chuckle, drawing her two sisters-in-law out of Leah's bedroom. "We'll see you at the church gathering."

The only ones left in the room were Ellie and *Mam*. Charlie had been up earlier, given her a hug, then promptly raced downstairs to help with last-minute details for the reception back at the house after the wedding ceremony.

"Is my hair *oll recht*?" Leah asked her mother. She was nervous, not a bad nervous, more like a tingling, warm, heightened anticipation of becoming Henry Yoder's wife.

It was early, before dawn. Leah had been amazed when the Lapp women arrived to help with the wedding feast before coming to her room to make sure she had everything she needed.

"Leah." Her mother's voice was hushed, reverent.

Leah met her gaze and saw tears in her *mam's* eyes. "What's wrong?"

Mam shook her head. "Nothing. Only that I'm going to miss having you at home."

She smiled. "We won't be far, and we'll come to visit often. So often that you'll get sick and tired of seeing us. And you can come to us. I'll make supper and when we have children, we'll want you to babysit and mother them." She bit her lip as she was overcome with emotion. "I love you. You've done so much for me."

"Nay," Mam whispered. "Not true. Loving you was easy, Leah. You were the sweetest and kindest little girl…and the loveliest young woman. I love you."

The two women hugged briefly. Ellie stood by with tears in her eyes.

Ready to wed the man she loved, Leah climbed into the buggy that would take her to the Lapps, where the church service and ceremony were to be held. It was a Tuesday. The November day promised to be clear if a bit chilly. Her cousin Isaac was driving while his wife, Ellen, sat next to him in the front seat. In the middle bench seat sat her older sister, Nell, and her brother-in-law James. Leah was with Henry in the vehicle's very back seat.

Henry clasped her hand and give it a reassuring squeeze. Leah met his loving gaze and couldn't stop the grin that settled on her lips. "You look beautiful, Leah," he whispered for her ears alone.

"I've never known anyone more handsome—inside and out." She chuckled when he arched his brows in puzzlement. "You're a wonderful man, Henry Yoder," she explained. "That's all I'm saying."

Then it was Henry's grin that lit up the back seat.

The church congregation had gathered in the Samuel Lapp residence. Henry's sister, Ruth, and family were among them. Even his brother, David, had arrived to surprise and please Henry and his parents. The front set of benches were for Henry and Leah in the center and their attendants on both sides of them.

Bishop John Fisher stood and asked Henry and Leah to step outside the room. He, Preacher Levi and the deacon, Abram Peachy, alternately spoke about marriage and their earthy duties as a couple and their responsibilities that the two of them would share in raising children. Leah blushed but nodded as she and Henry agreed with what was expected of them. Through the talk, they could hear the congregation singing wedding hymns from the *Ausbund*, the Amish book of hymns.

"Let's go back," the bishop said.

Leah felt the wonder of love as she accepted Henry as her husband. Henry was clearly more than happy to take her to be his wife. After a long sermon, Henry and she were called to step forward and asked to recite their vows as responses to a series of questions. Bishop John spoke without written word, straight from the heart and with the Lord's help.

"Are you willing to wed as God in the beginning ordained and commanded?" the bishop asked.

"Yes," Henry and Leah answered together.

"Henry, are you confident that God has chosen this sister to be your wedded wife?"

"Yes," Henry said with a glow in his eyes as he gazed at her.

"Leah, are you confident that God has chosen this brother to be your wedded husband?"

"Yes," Leah said as she beamed at Henry with greatly felt joy.

"Henry, do you promise before God and this church that you will never more depart from her, that you will care for and cherish her, even if bodily sickness comes to her or under any circumstances which a Christian husband is responsible to care for, until our dear God will again separate you from each other?"

"Yes."

Bishop John Fisher asked her and Henry to clasp hands before he gave the blessing over their marriage. Then the bishop pronounced them husband and wife.

Isaac and Ellen quickly pulled the newlyweds toward the carriage for the ride to the reception in the Arlin Stoltzfus home. Nell and James got into the seat in the middle, and Nell glanced back at them with a huge grin. "Welcome to the family, Henry."

Henry stared at his new sister-in-law and had never been happier than he was at that moment. "*Danki.* I'm pleased to be a member of your family," he murmured. As the others faced the front, he slipped his arm around

Leah's shoulders and pulled her to his side. "Mrs. Yoder, I love you."

Leah gazed at him, enrapt. "I like the sound of that. Mrs. Yoder, Mr. Yoder." She studied him silently. "I love you."

"Gut." He leaned close and kissed near her ear. "We're going to have many happy years together." He refused to let go of her, and he saw that she was pleased by his close proximity.

"We're almost there," Isaac called back. "Are you ready?"

The couple would be seated in the *eck*, one corner of the tables set up to form the shape of a squared-off U, with their attendants seated beside them.

"Will you mind living in the Yoder *haus*?" Henry asked his wife softly. His parents had decided to retire. They had given the store space over to Leah for her craft shop, which she decided to call Yoder's Country Crafts and Supplies. Harry and Margaret Yoder had moved into the *dawdi haus* in the back of the property, leaving the big house for Henry and Leah.

"I will love living in the Yoder big *haus*," she replied quietly. "I'm happy to live anyplace where you are." She bit her lip, and Henry felt the strongest urge to kiss her.

She was his wife, so he gave in to the feeling. "Leah," he breathed. When she turned to him, he kissed her and smiled when he saw her pink cheeks, bright eyes and the pretty curve of her lips afterward. "Wife."

"Husband." She leaned in closer. "Forever."

"Amen. *Forever,*" Henry whispered right before he stole another kiss from her.

* * * * *

If you loved this story,
check out the other books
in Rebecca Kertz's miniseries
WOMEN OF LANCASTER COUNTY

A SECRET AMISH LOVE
HER AMISH CHRISTMAS SWEETHEART

And don't forget to pick up these books
in her previous miniseries
LANCASTER COUNTY WEDDINGS

NOAH'S SWEETHEART
JEDIDIAH'S BRIDE
A WIFE FOR JACOB
ELIJAH AND THE WIDOW
LOVING ISAAC

Available now from Love Inspired!

Dear Reader,

I hope you've enjoyed visiting the Amish village of Happiness in Lancaster County, Pennsylvania. I love writing about all of the wonderful people who live there. In *Her Forgiving Amish Heart*, Leah Stoltzfus meets up again with Henry Yoder, her cousin's best friend. Henry got into a bit of trouble when he and Isaac were younger and on *rumspringa*, and he unintentionally hurt Isaac and others within his Amish community.

Leah never thought she'd marry. She'd never had a sweetheart or any man's attention. She'd resigned herself to the fact that she'd only have her craft shop in her future...until Henry shows her the possibilities of what it could be like to have more...

If you enjoyed *Her Forgiving Amish Heart*, you may want to try *A Secret Amish Love*, Leah's sister Nell's story, and *Her Amish Christmas Sweetheart*, about Leah and Nell's sister Meg, the middle daughter of Arlin and Missy Stoltzfus.

I hope you will continue to join me as I return time and again to Happiness where the Amish love, learn and raise children while being faithful to the Lord.

I wish you blessings, good health and much love.

Warmly,
Rebecca Kertz

COMING NEXT MONTH FROM **Love Inspired**®

Available July 17, 2018

A WIDOW'S HOPE

Indiana Amish Brides • by Vannetta Chapman

With her parents in danger of losing their home, widow Hannah King desperately needs a job. And carpenter—and old love—Jacob Schrock needs someone to put his business records in order. The last thing they both expect is a second chance at love.

HER COWBOY REUNION

Shepherd's Crossing • by Ruth Logan Herne

Widowed single dad Heath Caufield has too much on his plate when he inherits a share of Pine Ridge Ranch. And when his first love, Lizzie Fitzgerald, arrives to help run it, Heath knows he can't succeed without her. Can they forget the past and begin building a future?

THE RANCHER'S SURPRISE DAUGHTER

Colorado Grooms • by Jill Lynn

Lucas Wilder never thought he'd see his ex-girlfriend Cate Malory again—until she shows up insisting he has a three-year-old daughter. Determined to be part of the little girl's life, Lucas invites them to his family's dude ranch for the summer...and finds himself once again falling for Cate.

MEANT-TO-BE BABY

Rocky Mountain Haven • by Lois Richer

Army major Ben Adams didn't plan on becoming a father, but now he's suddenly guardian to his orphaned nephew. Asking soon-to-be mom Victoria Archer and her elderly aunts for advice seems like his best option—until he wishes Victoria could be by his side forever.

THE DEPUTY'S UNEXPECTED FAMILY

Comfort Creek Lawmen • by Patricia Johns

Officer Gabe Banks has never seen himself as the marriage-and-family type. But discovering he's the father of the little girl who bridal shop owner Harper Kemp is raising throws him for a loop. Now he'll have to figure out if he's willing to change his bachelor ways.

A FATHER FOR BELLA

by Jill Weatherholt

When real estate broker Joshua Carlson plans to buy the inn Faith Brennan manages, the widowed single mother intends to outbid him. But they soon learn working together may be the only way to reach their dreams of owning the inn *and* becoming a family.

LOOK FOR THESE AND OTHER LOVE INSPIRED BOOKS WHEREVER BOOKS ARE SOLD, INCLUDING MOST BOOKSTORES, SUPERMARKETS, DISCOUNT STORES AND DRUGSTORES.

LICNM0718

SPECIAL EXCERPT FROM

Love Inspired®

When a former sweetheart reappears in this widow's life, could it mean a second chance at love?

Read on for a sneak preview of
A Widow's Hope,
the first book in the series Indiana Amish Brides.

He knocked, and stood there staring when a young, beautiful woman opened the door. Chestnut-colored hair peeked out from her *kapp*. It matched her warm brown eyes and the sprinkling of freckles on her cheeks.

There was something familiar about her. He nearly smacked himself on the forehead. Of course she looked familiar, though it had been years since he'd seen her.

"Hannah? Hannah Beiler?"

"Hannah King." She quickly scanned him head to toe. She frowned and said, "I'm Hannah King."

"But…isn't this the Beiler home?"

"*Ya*. Wait. Aren't you Jacob? Jacob Schrock?"

He nearly laughed.

"The same, and I'm looking for the Beiler place."

"*Ya,* this is my parents' home, but why are you here?"

"To work." He stared down at the work order as if he could make sense of seeing the first girl he'd ever kissed standing on the doorstep of the place he was supposed to be working.

"I don't understand," he said.

"Neither do I. Who are you looking for?"

"Alton Beiler."

LIEXP0718

"But that's my father. Why—"

At that point Mr. Beiler joined them. "You're at the right house, Jacob. Please, come inside."

He'd never have guessed when he put on his suspenders that morning that he would be seeing Hannah Beiler before the sun was properly up. The same Hannah Beiler he had once kissed behind the playground.

Alton Beiler ushered Jacob into the kitchen.

"Claire, maybe you remember Jacob Schrock. Apparently he took our Hannah on a buggy ride once."

Jacob heard them, but his attention was on the young boy sitting at the table. He sat in a regular kitchen chair, which was slightly higher than the wheelchair parked behind him.

The boy cocked his head to the side, as if trying to puzzle through what he saw of Jacob. Then he said, *"Gudemariye."*

"And to you," Jacob replied.

"Who are you?" he asked.

"I'm Jacob. What's your name?"

"Matthew. This is Mamm, and that's Mammi and Daddi. We're a family now." Matthew grinned.

Hannah glanced at him and blushed.

"It's really nice to meet you, Matthew. I'm going to be working here for a few days."

"Working on what?"

Jacob glanced at Alton, who nodded once. "I'm going to build you a playhouse."

LIEXP0718